Marvel the Marvelous

MARVEL
THE MARVELOUS

LAURA CHESTER

Illustrated by

GARY A. LIPPINCOTT

WILLOW CREEK PRESS

Illustrations copyright © Gary Lippincott

With special thanks to my wonderful editor, Andrea Donner, as well as to some special friends, Leigh Moffat, Vanya Leitao, Tod Bowden, and Kathryn Miller. And with love to my husband, Mason Rose.

Editor: Andrea Donner

Published by Willow Creek Press
P.O. Box 147, Minocqua, Wisconsin 54548

Library of Congress Cataloging-in-Publication Data: On file

Printed in the U.S.A

for Kailer

Contents

Three Pink Ponies

*I*n the stable of the Ice Palace three pink ponies lived side by side, in three fine stalls made of burnished wood. When these three ponies went out for a run across the ice, little Marvel skated circles around the others.

Northern Joya was not a gloomy place. The high altitude brought one closer to the sun, and the dazzling light doubled on the mirror-like surfaces of the ice fields. Here in the far reaches of Northern Joya, most of the inhabitants wore skates, for without these sharp, silver blades, it would be too slippery to traverse the shimmering expanses.

In general, the inhabitants of Northern Joya were a happy lot. They often enjoyed homemade ice cream as well as a concoction of sweet slush, made from frozen violets. But the mainstay of the horses' diet was brittle feed, broken off from semi-frozen cubes in hard grey chunks.

Sometimes Marvel had strange dreams about green grass—fields to roll in, grass to munch on, rain-drenched, warm, fresh cut hay. She could almost smell its sweetness. But she didn't share this secret with her sisters who were both content and quite self-satisfied. They were happy being pink.

Marvel would have preferred almost any other color, but you are what you are, and you get what you get. She and her sisters had all sprung from three different blossoms on an iced-pink hollyhock. The oldest sister, Luster, arrived to greet the light of day two minutes before the second sister, Brilliance, who arrived thirty seconds before little Marvel.

Despite the close proximity of age, the three pink ponies always retained this order of superiority, (or inferiority, as some might say). Luster, being the tallest as well as the oldest, liked to look down her long elegant nose at her two younger siblings, or "*sublings,*" as she called them.

Behind her sisters' backs, the youngest pink pony whispered, "*First is worst, second the same, last the best of all the game!*" Then she'd prance around in glee, posing on the sharp teeth of her figure skates. She liked to skate very fast and then cut to a sharp stop, spraying a fantail of ice chips just for fun.

Luster thought this exhibitionism not worthy of encouragement, for Marvel was always rushing about so, mussing up her mane and matting her golden forelock. Luster felt that Marvel's antics didn't improve their status in Joya. She was too unruly, an unpolished pink. How would they ever meet any nice stallions with such riff-raff running around?

Luster was known for her silky platinum mane and tail. She also had perfect proportions, and enjoyed a daily inspection of herself, which was easy enough to do, considering the fact that the ice surrounding them was as reflective as a mirror.

Brilliance, the middle pony, often called "Brince," had a

mahogany-colored mane and tail. But she was as slow on her feet as she was fast in her mind. She walked gingerly, and preferred to keep her mane neatly braided and out of the way, believing that the tight red-brown braids helped her to focus, to concentrate.

Brince liked to ponder every situation, every nuance and proclamation from every possible angle. It could be dizzying for poor little Marvel to follow her *chew-chew* train of thought. But it was even more dizzying for Brilliance to watch Marvel dashing about like some kind of dervish.

Little Marvel, the youngest, rarely groomed herself, but most of the creatures in Northern Joya thought that she was the prettiest pink pony of all, though they wouldn't dare say so, for fear of offending the two older sisters. Little Marvel's mane and tail were a luscious gold even if a bit wild looking.

"I AM wild," she proclaimed.

Marvel didn't have time for complaints or worries, gossip or slander. She was too busy carving pictures in the ice.

Despite Little Marvel's special gifts, her older sisters liked to point out her failings—that she was impetuous, whatever that was supposed to mean, and kept the messiest stall and never polished her blades. Big deal!

In turn, Marvel complemented them on how beautifully they kept themselves and their nice, neat stalls. "I'm sorry I'm not a bit tidier, but what's the point, really?"

She appreciated a clean stall as much as anyone, but it seemed to get messy in no time, and one could spend one's entire life cleaning things up, and she had much better things to do than primp, preen and pamper herself in the confines of a box stall! What's the point of polishing your skates when blades are dull in a day?

"I doubt if I'll ever change," Marvel admitted. "Horses are born the way they are, and change only comes in pinches."

With this proclamation she gave a little buck, and went racing across the ice fields. Nobody could catch her.

Marvel didn't care much for argument. Whenever there was a quarrel amongst the three pink ponies, it was Marvel who tried to keep harmony amongst them, saying— "We have to play together, not fight each other."

Brilliance, who was very well read, corrected her. "Play is not the important thing—everyone knows that work is what we should be doing. We all have to *work* together, like three strands of a single braid, made strong by being woven together, clasped at the bottom with a single cord."

"Yes, Unity!" replied Little Marvel, not wishing to expend so much brain power in following that scenario. She preferred a rhyme when it came to making sense, or nonsense for that matter.

"*Three against three is not for me. Three for One is much more fun.*"

"Number One, are you referring to me?" asked Luster, tossing her platinum mane back and forth over her slender shoulders.

But Little Marvel had actually been thinking about the One and Only golden Pink Cloud of Perfection, wondering when it would appear in Northern Joya again, bringing happiness and opalites along with the sweet smell of cut apples.

Whenever it arrived, the golden Pink Cloud left the entire population very still, yet exuberant. It made Little Marvel think of a hummingbird's heart, the whirring of its wings—all stirred up, but suspended in the air—perfectly still, yet full of life! It made her incredibly happy. The mysterious Pink Cloud appeared in Joya irregularly, and it was only the youngest pony who was able to hear what the Pink Cloud said.

I wonder why it doesn't speak to me, thought Brilliance, since I'm the intelligent one.

Luster thought the golden Pink Cloud should have been attracted to her, since the shine of her coat resembled the sparkles of the mysterious, heavenly cloud. But they had to admit that Marvel had a gift for listening, and only she could interpret what the Pink Cloud said.

As if Little Marvel had sensed it coming, that evening around sunset, the golden Pink Cloud came tumbling across the sky, flashing with silent lightning and radiant-colored opalites. It hovered above the Ice Palace and all the creatures became intensely still.

Little Marvel listened carefully, but all she could discern was this message—*Special visitors coming soon. Prepare yourselves. Be true.*

The older sisters didn't think that was much of a prophecy. Couldn't Marvel be more specific? How were they supposed to prepare themselves? Should they have their manes combed out or braided? Should they prepare a feast or begin a diet?

But Little Marvel said that that was all the translation she could give, though she did sense that it was going to be a very *unusual* visit. "We should start getting ready now!"

"Where should we start?" Luster retorted. "Inside the stable or out?"

Inside your heart, thought Marvel.

In response to the prediction, all the creatures of Northern Joya tried to prepare themselves. Garbonzo the giant mastiff, and his little pug friend, Beanie, thought they should tidy the Ice Palace grounds. The two dogs guarded the Palace gates though there had been little to guard for quite some time.

They were incredibly eager, and began to practice maneuvers, marching around the castle walls, first this way, then that

way, up and down, left to right. They did not need to wear skates, because their scritchy-scratchy nails dug into the ice and kept them steady on their feet.

Once in a while the pug's toenails grew so long, they became like little black circles, and then he slid around on the ice, as if he were walking on marbles. He hated to have his toenails cut, but when they got very long, Garbonzo had to hold him down with a paw and clip the curling toenails off.

Luster, being the most keen on the looks of things, was in charge of the beautification program, while Brilliance tried to figure out what would be the optimum day in the solar year for a special visit of such magnitude.

While they were busy with their chores, Little Marvel began carving a *Welcome* sign in a slope of ice with her sharpened skates, and all the animals had to admit that she did an especially beautiful job of embellishing the capital *W* with a sprinkling of ice flowers and carved-out stars.

Every night as the three pink ponies nestled down in the straw of their stable, Garbonzo and Beanie would trot on down for a visit. The pug dearly loved to chat, and Garbonzo didn't like to guard the Ice Palace gates alone, so he followed the smaller, yappier dog.

"Brince, do you think it might happen tomorrow?" Beanie asked the smartest pony, but Brilliance shook her head, *No.* She had calculated the position of the stars and figured that the visit would occur in a fortnight.

"What's a fortnight?" the pug dog asked.

17

"Two weeks, or more specifically—fourteen days," Brilliance tried to explain, by making marks in the snow with the polished blade of her skate. She didn't have much patience for the mastiff or the pug—they seemed dim-witted to her, but they were special friends of Marvel's, so Brilliance obliged them with answers.

"I thought a fort knight would be a soldier, with cannons and guns," the mastiff imagined, knowing that Brilliance was probably right, as she always seemed to be.

"*Fourteen days of anticipation, fourteen days of preparation!*" Little Marvel neighed, for she loved to have something to look forward to—any exciting change.

And who could tell what the visitors might bring—sugar perhaps, or a bucket of warm mash!

"Perhaps they'll bring ribbons," Luster imagined.

"Or carrots to improve our minds," Brince said.

Bonzo suspected that the visitors might be dangerous enemies in disguise, and they should all be on their guard. Being on guard was his nature, so no one took his apprehension seriously. He could take on the job of worrying for them all.

The next morning another day was crossed off the calendar, and the whole crew was so full of excitement, that they decided to have a race to the top of the highest peak. They all wanted to be in good shape for when the special visitors arrived.

Scrambling and panting and pawing up to the summit, Beanie yipped "*I'm last!*" He then stood there bowing in the most fetching manner, while Little Marvel whispered to him, "*First is worst, second the same.* That makes us *best* of ALL the game!"

"Why do you always say that?" Brilliance wanted to know, annoyed by this silly, senseless rhyme. "Why in all the land of Joya do you think the last one could possibly be *best*? That's the stupidest thing I've ever heard."

"Maybe the dumb ones will be smart someday," suggested Beanie.

"Don't hold your breath," said Luster.

A host of Snowdrops, small bell-like flowers, who adorned the fields of the north country, stayed behind and didn't race, for they didn't care much for competition. They would rather huddle together and think about hope—hope for spring, hope for melting, hope for warmer weather.

Their soft puff-breaths melted wee patches around their dainty skirts, and allowed bits of earth to peek through the ice,

but they never had succeeded in melting the snowfields that covered the expanse of Northern Joya. That would take a field of Sunflowers, and they had never come this far north.

A fortnight went by quite rapidly. The Pink Ponies were making every effort to look their best, which was a bit of a struggle for Marvel, though she did agree to polish her blades, and submitted to her sisters' grooming. *OUCH!*

What she really wanted to do was to roll in the dirt, if she could only find some nice dark dirt in this snow-clean country. Luster and Brince held their youngest sibling by the halter and combed her unruly mane, pulling at her golden tail until it hung just so. She certainly did look fabulous, but everyone knew it wouldn't last.

Still, Beanie *Ohhed* and Garbanzo *Ahhed.* "You could be a circus pony!" cried Beanie. "You could be on some kind of postcard!"

"If only you would keep it that way," Luster sighed, but Little Marvel was afraid she'd have to stay in her stall and stand stock still if she was going to remain "*that way.*"

"Forget it," she cried, dashing off. They could always brush her down again later—so off she went, out into the wind where her thick mane quickly tangled and her forelock stood straight up.

Luster brought out a silver blanket from her shiny tack box and aired it in the mountain breeze, polishing the hardware that clasped the blanket to her chest. A crisscrossing, double belt fastened the covering around her slender belly. She really looked stupendous, though Garbonzo whispered to Beanie, "Looks a bit like a party pony with no particular place to go."

Brince asked the doves to help re-braid her hair. The activity of braiding came naturally to them, as they liked to weave things together. They even wove in a few of their own white feathers at the end, and *cooed* in admiration. Brince made a deep equine bow and felt very bright indeed!

On the eve of the thirteenth day there was a special feeling of anticipation, and sure enough, that evening, just as the sun was setting, spreading its glory over the mountainous skies, the golden Pink Cloud appeared on the horizon again, twinkling and billowing, until it spread over the entire kingdom, leaving a wonderful hush and apple-like aroma.

Everyone remained perfectly still so that Little Marvel could hear what the Pink Cloud had to say now. But all the youngest pony could hear was the sound of tinkling silver bells, jingling and jangling, coming, it seemed, from a very great distance. Little Marvel didn't know what that meant, but the bells seemed to be getting closer and closer, and that seemed to be a good sign.

"Maybe it's an Ice Cream truck," cried Beanie, for he adored ice cream, vanilla with caramel swirls, *yum yum*.

"Maybe..." Garbonzo paused, "maybe it's only a disguise of some sort, to throw us off the track."

"Maybe it's a herd of reindeer!" Luster thought, "bringing us a load of presents!"

"We'll just have to wait and see," said Marvel. "Only the Pink Cloud knows for sure."

The ponies tried to stay up all night to greet the new arrivals, but one by one, they fell asleep.

Hours later they woke to Beanie's yipping. "Fortnight fortnight! Read all about it!"

Brilliance had to explain to him that *today* could not be the fortnight, because a fortnight was always fourteen days away.

22

"Confusing," Bonzo admitted, chewing on his old bone, because chewing helped to calm him, and made him less suspicious.

"Will you please put that gruesome chunk of anatomy out of our sight," Luster told him. "You can't be gnawing and slobbering when our guests arrive. It's disgusting."

Bonzo sorrowfully tucked the bone behind him. He didn't like to be told what to do, especially by a little pink pony, but he also wanted to do the right thing, and exhibit proper behavior. "We are royal dogs after all," he told Beanie.

"We are?" Beanie said, not quite sure what that meant, though he had a vague recollection of sitting on someone's comfortable, royal lap, with his friend, Garbonzo, at the regal feet of another.

"We keep the best company," Bonzo added, hoping that Luster would overhear.

"How do you keep a company?" Beanie asked. "Do you dig a hole and then bury it?"

"Too many questions," Bonzo replied. "It muddles me."

"I am accompanied!" the little pug danced. "*A company dog. Not a frog. A hippity-hoppity-skippity dog.*"

Just at that moment, in the snowy distance, they all heard jingle bells approaching. From far away and around the bend— the sound was clearly growing louder.

Brilliance instructed the three white doves to fly out and see what was coming. Away they went, weaving over the ice fields until they were out of sight.

"I better take up my position," said Bonzo. "Come on, Beanie. Let's be on guard."

The little pug reluctantly left the party of ponies and went to join his friend at the Ice Palace gate.

"We have a good vantage point from here," said Bonzo.

"Advantage? Over whom?"

"Sit still. I mean—Attention! Get ready to salute. And try to look your smartest."

"I'm *not* stupid," the pug replied. "I'm just a wee, weenie bit curious. And I can't sit still when I'm excited." He started to spin, then leapt up and down on his freshly cut toenails to demonstrate his state of mind, aggravating the larger dog.

"If you are going to hop around like that, why don't you go greet whomever it is that's coming. And try not to yap too much. It annoys."

Given permission, Beanie went skittering down a very steep, slippery slope, and went plunging across a snowfield where he quickly sank up to his tummy and could not move at all. The Snowdrops had to come and melt him out.

After being dragged to safety, he lay down and sulked—"I'm tired of all this snow." With his dark little face on his paws he looked so miserable everyone had to laugh, even Garbonzo, and that made Beanie bark and bark as if to scold them all.

New Arrivals

*T*he jingle bells grew louder and louder and the three pink ponies all danced in a ring, practicing their welcoming moves.

"The white doves are coming," the mastiff barked, and sure enough, two of the snow white birds were flying back with long white glistening streamers, making a heart shape, over and over, while the third dove flew through the middle holding a small red rose.

"Look," cried Beanie. "A Sign of Life!"

"Spring!" cheered the Snowdrops.

"What could it mean?" neighed Luster.

Brilliance tried to figure it out. "It must be a symbol of something." But she didn't have a chance to finish pondering, for the Snowdrops were ringing their bells so loudly it drowned out every form of sensible thought.

"Put on your very best face!" Luster whinnied, holding her head up high.

Little Marvel leapt up and down for joy as a beautiful blue sleigh appeared on the horizon, pulled by two powerful horses—giant white Lippizans. They wore steel crampons on their hooves, spikes that dug deeply into the ice, and made the pulling of their load look easy. They were so enormous it was hard to tell who was in the sleigh behind them.

Bonzo, sitting up at his perfect vantage point, got the first real look. When he saw who it was, he barked—"The King! THE ROYAL COUPLE!"

"Just as I thought," muttered Brilliance.

"There's somebody in between them, though," Beanie snorted, panting in circles, for he wanted everyone to know that he had been observant. Plus, he hated to be ignored.

"But they are not wearing their crowns," said Luster in astonishment. "I wonder what happened to their crowns?"

"Probably stolen along the path," Garbanzo declared, though no one bothered to listen to his suspicions. Still, the assembly as a whole was more than a little bit shocked. Why were the King and Queen returning to the Ice Palace without their crowns?

"Maybe they are imposters," Bonzo dared to say, but the three white doves cooed—"*Nooo, nooo-nooo*," assuring the ponies that it *was* the Royal Couple, as well as a very sad girl.

"Looks like a sourpuss," Beanie said, making a dour expression as well, which was easy enough for him to do.

One look from Little Marvel reminded Beanie that it wasn't nice to call anyone names, especially a new arrival.

All the animals gathered around the sleigh to bid the Royal Couple welcome. But Beanie was the first to notice the two thin lines of melted ice that had appeared where the runners had passed. The little pug put his nose to the ground, sniffed and chortled and began to dig. "*Oh MY!* Delicious—MUD!"

Marvel came over to inspect the lovely mud, too. She had to restrain herself from digging it up with her hoof. She had a very strong impulse to get down on the ground and roll all around in it, making a mess of her coat.

Now that the sleigh had finally come to a standstill, the three pink ponies almost forgot themselves and their pleasing plan of welcome. The two older sisters were smitten with the big white Lippizans. The pink polish of their coats became even rosier as they giggled and blushed and swayed about on their skates as if they might swoon and tumble over.

The Queen stood up and waved, "*Ta-ta!* We're here, my Darling Dears, and over such a distance!"

The King almost fell out of the sleigh, kicking off layers of woolen blankets, and the grim little girl sat perfectly still, sniffling and snuffling, as if she had a headache AND a very bad cold.

"As you can see we have left our crowns behind," the Queen explained.

"We melted them down, you know," the King continued— "*Hear hear!* So here and there and so forth. No more pontification. We're finished with all of that, you know."

"Ponty-*what*?" barked Beanie, as he came up to sniff the skirt of the Queen. It did smell wonderfully nice and familiar. The Queen seemed delighted to see her little pug dog, and bent down to pick him up, but Beanie scampered away, and she laughed, for he was such an imp!

"You are still our Dearly Beloveds," sang out the Queen. "And we hope you feel the same way!"

All the Snowdrops clapped and spun about to demonstrate their total affection and absolute loyalty.

The Queen proceeded to throw kisses to everyone, and as she did so, little white butterflies wafted up into the air landing here and there—on the lips and noses and eyebrows of all the creatures. One even bounced on the curly tail of the pug.

Little Marvel went and bowed before the King, which seemed to charm him no end. The King gave Marvel a long, lingering pat on the head. "You'll be happy to know," the King said gruffly, "that we built you a Treasure House. You must come and see it someday. Can't stay up here in the cold forever."

Marvel shook her head up and down, for she liked the sound of an adventure.

"What's a Treasure House?" Beanie inquired. "Can you go inside? Can you live there?"

"Maybe if you listened, you'd find out," scolded Brince, though even she was not sure what a Treasure House was; not having the exact information always made her anxious.

"We came all this way to invite you," the Queen added, stepping out onto the frozen tundra. "But what a grand skating rink you have! As far as the eye can *see-see-see.*" She made a little salute like a sailor and all the creatures saluted her back, which made her clap her hands in delight.

"And who have you brought with you?" Beanie yapped, for he couldn't contain his curiosity another single instant. "Who *is* that grumpy person?"

Garbonzo cuffed him away from the sleigh. It wasn't proper for royal dogs to go poking their noses into everyone's business, but the Queen was not offended, nor was the child who seemed oblivious to them anyway.

"Oh yes, indeed, our funny little guest." The Queen rubbed her hands together, as if to make some heat, and then turned to introduce the foundling. "This dear child has not given us her name, for I'm afraid she is *very* worried and thoroughly chilled. We plucked her out of a snowbank. Probably a visitor from the other side," she whispered to Brince who was exceedingly attentive.

"She was almost frozen solid," added the King. "And I don't believe she has thawed out yet, for she has not uttered one single syllable!"

"Shall we breathe on her," the Snowdrops asked?

"We had better heat her up slowly," Brince responded, for she knew all about boiling and freezing and thawing, and you don't want to thaw someone out too quickly—that could be very painful.

It was true, the child was extremely cold. Her lips were blue and she was shivering. Even her tears had frozen on her cheeks. And there was frost on her eyelashes, icicles hanging from her golden hair.

"She is in a very low mood," the Queen confided in Luster. Perhaps the Queen was hoping that Luster might take charge, not realizing that Luster primarily took care of herself and herself alone.

Luster simply shrugged, glancing over at the huge white Lippizans, giving them an inviting toss of her platinum mane. She had better things to think about than a frozen child.

"There's nothing like a little mountain sunshine to *lift* a person Up!" the Queen cried, throwing her hands up into the air, and all the Snowdrops did the same, creating a momentary, balmy breeze.

It was a radiant (though freezing), sparkling day—the light almost bounced off the ice fields, but the little girl's eyes looked glazed over, as if she saw nothing, nothing at all.

Little Marvel was concerned, and determined to find out the child's full name. Perhaps talking would help bring her back to life. Marvel went up to the sleigh, and stretched out her neck to nuzzle the girl, as if teasing for a tiny tidbit. Marvel didn't understand tears, but when she nuzzled closer, she found that they tasted like salt! "Delicious," Marvel whinnied, but the child only sobbed once, in response, frowning to make your heart break.

Marvel persisted, and put her velvety nose out, breathing warm puffs on the girl's cold hands, nuzzling her in the gentlest manner. Then she tried a rhyme—that usually helped to cheer people up. "*Howdy stranger. You're out of danger. Are you a stone, or a lone park ranger?*"

Finally the girl child looked at Marvel for the first time and in an icy little voice she whispered, "Strange place."

Marvel was secretly excited that the girl had spoken, and wanting to encourage her to go on. "Look! You and I have the exact same hair! Real gold. What do you think?"

The child looked at the little pink pony who was standing there before her, and then tilted her head. It looked as if she were about to smile, but instead she pulled off her hat, and her tangle of icy hair clattered with dangling icicles. Her big blue eyes grew even bigger and her face looked frozen through.

The Snowdrops all came and huddled about the frozen girl. They huffed and puffed with their warmest breaths—but it only served to defrost the tips of her fingers.

Marvel breathed on her hands a bit more, and the little girl made her fingers wiggle, but then she cried and said it hurt too much. She wished that she had been left in the snowbank where she hadn't felt a thing.

But then she grew quiet and listened intently. "Do you hear that? Do you hear a baby crying? It sounds so far away."

Beanie stood up on his hind legs and wiggled his paws, and said that he didn't hear '*nuthin*'. None of them did. But it was clear that the girl had heard something. Beanie cocked his head and pretended to hear, first on this side, then on that.

"Don't tease," the mastiff told the pug, though the girl child looked like she was about to smile. Instead, she sniffed a bit and sat quite still. Perhaps she was afraid that her face might break into a million pieces if she let herself smile, and she had to hold herself together with a terrible effort.

The child's sadness was contagious. Soon all of the Snow-drops began to shake off the frozen drops that had accumulated on their leaves, and they clattered about and made everyone slip and slide.

Even the King went glissading and landed on his royal rump. He shouted, "*Rats,*" whereupon the little girl finally cracked a glimmer of a smile.

"I saw it first! I saw it," barked Beanie. His excitement put him into a kind of snuffling-snorting fit.

The girl child gazed in the pug's direction, and finally asked, "Do you think his breathing will improve?"

This sent them all into fresh peals of laughter.

Little Marvel nuzzled the child's arm a bit to get her attention, and the girl responded by putting one hand under Marvel's golden mane where it was nice and warm.

"Don't be sad," said Marvel. "You're safe with us now. You'll thaw."

But she didn't look like she quite believed this. She turned to her new friend with the golden mane and said, "I do believe I'm dead."

"*Dead*," Marvel whispered. "What do you mean by *dead*?"

"You know, not alive," the girl child whispered.

Marvel didn't want Brilliance to overhear this, or they might get a lecture or an explanation, and that could be so tedious.

"You look quite alive to me."

The girl child was not convinced.

Thawing Out the Child

"*B*ut everything is changed," Lee said. "I don't know where I am. I don't think I belong here."

"You're in the land of Joya now, Northern Joya to be exact."

The child didn't respond to this. She was trying hard to remember something. She shook her head, as if she could shake the memory loose. "I think we were driving to Gramma's. We were going for Sunday supper."

She paused, for she was thinking about the car, and the last moment she could remember—"I know my parents were up in front," she began, extremely slowly, as if seeing things through a fog. "My mother was nursing the baby, and my brother and I were fighting over sides."

"Sides? What do you mean by sides?" Beanie asked. He had calmed down a bit and was now breathing normally.

"Sides, in the backseat, you know, the line that divides my

side from his. He hit me whenever I moved into his territory," she explained.

"*Hmmm*," Marvel thought, that sounded familiar—this side, that side, first/last, worst/best—it happened like that everywhere all-the-time, and got everyone into trouble.

"*She's breathing up all my air!* my brother yelled, and then the baby started to cry and my father jammed on the brakes and tried to reach around and smack us, but then the car... the car.."

LEEZIE, PUT YOUR HEAD DOWN!

Lee put her hand on her head and covered her eyes as if she were still dizzy. Then she sat up trembling.

"There was a terrible *bang*, and I was shooting through space—stars and moons were flying by all around me. Then finally, there was this enormous jolt and I ended up in that snowbank. I don't even know where my parents are, or if our baby is still alive. Why wasn't my brother in the snowbank with me? If I hadn't put my hand over onto his side, none of this would have happened."

"It sounds like you were in an accident, but that you got saved," Marvel offered. "Maybe the Pink Cloud protected you."

"Well, if it was watching out for me, why did it let me freeze?"

"Only the Pink Cloud knows for sure," Marvel answered, and Beanie added his two cents:

"Maybe you had to wait for the King and Queen to come along, and the Pink Cloud knew they would save you, and bring you here to Northern Joya, where we would all meet and become best friends!"

All of that sounded perfectly logical to Marvel, but Leezie didn't think so. "The sleigh did come," she answered. "They were very kind and threw tons of blankets over me, and sang me songs, and tried to give me sips of something I couldn't really swallow... I just don't understand where my brother is."

"I'm sure he's fine," Beanie responded. "Aren't you hungry?" he asked, because he was almost always thinking about food.

Lee shrugged. She was still picturing her home on earth—her comfortable bed, and their kitchen table. How would she ever get back there? She thought briefly of their Sunday waffle breakfasts, with real maple syrup, and good fresh milk from the local farm. They always had skillet browned sausages too. Breakfast was her favorite meal.

"So, what do you like to do on earth?" Little Marvel asked, trying to change the subject.

Lee thought about that for a moment. "I love my stuffed animal collection. They sleep with me." She realized that she missed cuddling up with them, talking to them and telling them secrets, playing all sorts of games under the covers.

"We have lots of animals here to keep you company," Marvel assured her. "I bet even Beanie would volunteer to cuddle up with you. He looks a bit like a stuffed potato."

"Don't volunteer *me* for duty!" cried Beanie.

But Lee was still thinking about the comforts of home and her neighborhood, where all the kids had flying saucers and drank hot chocolate after school, and how she loved to make a stack of Ritz crackers with peanut butter in between umpteen slices. She realized now that she was very hungry! But what did they have to eat in such a frozen place as this?

More importantly, there was something else occupying her troubled mind. "Your Queen said that if I visited the Treasure House, I might be able to get home."

"Where's home?" barked Beanie, twirling around and around. He felt at home wherever he found himself. "Can you spell it out for a sausage?"

But Lee did not pay him much attention. She was still thinking about the Treasure House. "Do you know where it is? Have you been there?"

Marvel shook her head, no. "I've never been anywhere, just all around here."

"Around and around and *around*!" barked Beanie, continuing to twirl.

"The Treasure House is probably on the other side of Joya. I've never been there myself, but maybe it's not too far. After all, the King and Queen came in their sleigh. I may not be a big white Lippizan, but I can still cover a lot of miles!"

"Will you take me?" she asked. "Can we go there?" Lee suddenly had so much to say. The color was definitely returning to her cheeks and it made her look quite pretty.

Little Marvel had never been to the warm side of Joya, and she knew very little about this Treasure House, but the youngest pink pony was always up for an adventure. "We'll go. I promise, sometime soon. But first you had better recover, and I'm afraid that means some sustenance. We have to make plans and draw up a map and pack provisions and get you some skates."

Lee Rumsey was satisfied with this. It was only a matter of time. She placed one hand on Marvel's neck and carefully descended from the sleigh. Quickly, it became apparent that she could not traverse the ice fields very well in rubber boots.

"Not well equipped," said Brilliance, trotting up. "Let me think of a solution."

"We could drag her," Beanie suggested, as he came skidding over to investigate. But "dragging" didn't sound like a nice way to treat a brand new guest. He gave her a sniff with his little mashed mug face and wiggled his curly tail, which made Lee smile, but he wouldn't let her pat him. "Not so fast!"

Brilliance concluded that what they needed was a child-size sled—so she trotted off to look for one inside the Ice Palace. But all she could come up with was a laundry basket. It looked like it might do. With a long cord attached to the handle, it became a suitable means of transport. Lee climbed in and sat right down in the middle of a clean, unfolded load of laundry. Holding onto the handles of the basket, they were off to join the others, with Beanie yapping along behind.

The King and Queen had both brought their high-laced skates to help support their elderly ankles. Holding hands, they teetered across the ice field, and then began to dance together. The King was easily winded, and needed the Queen's help. She finally got him settled squarely on a lump of ice they referred to as "His Throne."

The Queen then went off to practice her figure 8's, still remarkably agile, even at her age. No one knew what that might be, though Brilliance figured it was probably somewhere around one-hundred-and-eleven.

"*One and one and one,*" sang the Snowdrops, "*And look—she still has fun!*"

But when all was said and done, the Queen seemed truly ageless. She swung her arms to help her make her figure 8's, and all the Snowdrops spun in circles and rang out their admiration.

Garbonzo came up to the foot of the ice throne and asked the King in a hushed sort of voice, "So what do you think—is this traveler a friend or a foe?"

"You never know, you never know," the King responded, for he shared Garbonzo's suspicious nature.

"She might have been put there as a decoy," Garbonzo suggested as the Queen skated up.

"Our main concern should be," added the Queen—"how are we to cheer this dear child up? She is *very* morose!"

Hearing this, all the Snowdrops began their ding-a-ling song, which pleased the Queen no end. "*Ding we sing, din-a-ling, ding-a-dong, come sing with us and join our song!*"

"Wonderful, wonderful!" the good Queen cheered. "We must have more music, especially during dinner."

"And with our mouths full!" Beanie snorted, for he liked exhibiting bad table manners and breaking every rule.

The Snowdrops clamored around the Queen, *dinging* and *donging*, as if they were longing to announce a feast.

"Bring that girl in the basket, and let's eat up!" shouted the King.

"Her name is not *that girl*," Beanie corrected.

They all waited for her to speak. Marvel had to nudge her once, and whisper—"Time for introductions."

"Me?" she asked, "Oh yes. My name is Lee, Lee Rumsey."

"*Ooooooo*," they all whistled in unison.

"She's from the other side," muttered Garbonzo.

"The other side of what?" she questioned.

"You know, like a glove turned inside out," Beanie answered. "We're on the inside."

"Oh," she responded. *The Inside.*

So that was settled, and they all streamed up toward the Ice Palace courtyard, where a welcoming feast had been prepared—platters of delicious morsels warmed in the wintry sun. There was even a goblet of chilled ice wine, but just for the Royal Couple.

All Lee could say was, "This certainly is a very cold *inside*," with very cold utensils. She was afraid her fingers would stick to her fork. "Do you always eat everything frozen?"

"If you got some exercise," Brilliance advised, "you would warm up in no time, for molecules in motion make significant heat."

With that, Little Marvel sped off across the ice field with Lee hanging on inside the laundry basket. When Marvel turned, the basket flew out in a wide circle and the little girl shrieked with glee.

Finally when Marvel came to a stop, the basket kept going, jerking the little pink pony around. The girl child laughed, and Little Marvel noticed that Lee's cheeks looked very rosy indeed, and all the icicles had melted from her hair. Her eyes had gone from a frozen grey, to a sparkling blue. It was also true, that Leezie's mane of wild gold curls was the exact same shade as Marvel's. They were sure to become best friends.

Leezie Builds a Fire

A little nourishment brought even more color back into Leezie's cheeks. She hadn't eaten in the longest time. It seemed like forever and a day.

The last thing she remembered was a cherry-flavored Tootsie Roll Pop. She had just been getting to the chewy part when her brother gave her a punch, and it dropped from her mouth onto the dirty floor of the car. Of course she screamed, which made the baby cry, which made her mother upset, which made her father mad, which made him reach around to swat her brother, which made the car spin out of control.

She then remembered there was freezing sleet and the car was sliding on a patch of ice and a truck was coming toward them—"*Stop!*"

Lee covered her face and Marvel responded by standing very still. Marvel didn't understand death, or the past, but they all knew they had to get this golden child to think more about the here and now. She seemed to be stuck in a bad dream.

"We have cherry-flavored icicles here in Joya," Beanie offered, but Lee shook her head, no. She wanted a cup of hot chocolate, preferably with fresh whipped cream, and a stack of Ritz crackers with peanut butter, or at the very least some buttered popcorn.

"Yeah, *right*," Garbonzo muttered.

All of the creatures looked at each other, because they didn't really know about these foods. They were used to eating cool or cold or *semi-fredo*—shaved ice, or slush, or rock hard.

"Do you have any sticks?" asked the girl, for she had an idea. But the animals of Joya looked a bit baffled.

"You know, wood, small branches from a tree—kindling."

"Is that like—next of kin?" asked Beanie.

Brilliance didn't think so.

"I bet *you* have a looking glass," Leezie said to Luster, who trotted off to find a mirror she had tucked away in her tack room chest.

The King and Queen had settled down on their icy thrones to watch the goings-on as if it were a spectacle meant to amuse them.

"We no longer feel in charge, you know," the King admitted to Garbonzo, who lay at the King's feet just as he used to. It made Bonzo feel very happy to have the King back home, crown or no crown, for he was still the same old King with the same royal smell—a mixture of lime and rose soap, mint and cherry pipe tobacco.

Brilliance produced two dry sticks that had been tucked away in the Palace parlor for knitting up scarves and mittens. "I do believe these are made out of wood."

But then Lee asked for paper, another commodity that was somewhat scarce.

Beanie dashed into the Palace and found a notepad and proceeded to crumple up page after page. He had the greatest fun tearing and tossing. "Think," he said to Marvel—"I won't even get scolded for making a mess!"

"Now, do you have any logs?" Lee continued to make requests. She was certainly coming back to life, it seemed. "You know, I mean—like timbers."

"Is she suggesting we they tear the Ice Palace down?" Brilliance queried.

But the Queen insisted that the fire was necessary and they

should do whatever they had to do. "We shall have a proper bonfire! *Ta-ta!—Quite big, not small, for One and All!*"

"Fires most likely inspire," Brilliance agreed, though she hid the fact that she didn't really know what a bonfire looked like.

Marvel went to help the others drag old timbers from the walls of the crumbling Ice Palace, while her two older sisters went off swishing their tails around the big white Lippizans.

As the supporting structure was taken away, the Palace itself began to fall into a pile of gigantic ice cubes.

"You can't have everything," clapped the Queen. "And we can always build an igloo!" She was in one of her extremely jolly moods.

"We can sleep in the sleigh if it comes to that," said the King. It didn't sound as if they intended to stay very long.

"Will you be here for a fortnight?" asked Beanie, wanting to use the word at least one more time.

"Perhaps," said the Queen.

Hearing this the little Snowdrops hung their heads and looked like they might collapse upon their stems.

"Please stand up," Brince told the flowers. "The child is going to rub her sticks together, and we need everyone to concentrate. Luster, will you hold the looking glass, please?"

Lee felt a new urgency in her every move, as if each thing she did brought her closer to home. She thought she heard her baby sister crying in the distance, and it made her want to get going.

Lee made a small pile of crumpled paper, then built a little teepee of kitchen spoons above. With the looking glass reflect-

ing the strong mountain light right on the spot where she twee-
dled and turned the two knitting needles—soon a spark ignited
and the paper burst into flame—then the smaller pieces of wood
were tossed on top, and up the fire roared. With the timbers
added, the blaze became a virtual bonfire, and the entire kingdom was dazzled. They had never felt anything so warm! And
it made them rather dizzy. Some began to waltz.

The two older sisters felt that the fire was terribly romantic
and it emboldened Luster to approach the Lippizans, and con-
vince them to take off their harnesses and have some fun.

"Do you know how to dance?" Luster asked the more dig-
nified horse.

The big white Lippizan nearly bellowed. Then he went on
to boast that it was a well known fact that Lippizans were the
ballet dancers of the horse kingdom.

"Really?" Luster blushed. She was impressed that such a
massive creature could also be an agile dancer. He did have a
very athletic physique. She swished her platinum tail at him and
trotted off as if to entice. He took the lead, and followed right
after, until they were standing shoulder to shoulder watching the
fire burn.

Brilliance was not an expert at flirtation, but she concluded
that perhaps if she unbraided her hair she would have a bit
more appeal. So she solicited the help of two white doves, and
soon her mahogany-colored mane was rippling over her shoulders. The second Lippizan also seemed smitten. He came and
stood beside her.

Brilliance's mind was all a-boggle. She didn't know what to say. She didn't quite like her emotions being so out of control. "Do you like to read?" she asked the big white horse.

"I'd rather prance," he responded, and before she knew what was happening to her, she was being flung up into the air—tossed and caught, and even nibbled along the neck—for that is the way that horses kiss.

"Disgusting," Marvel thought. Those Lippizans were so full of themselves. She'd rather play with the pug.

"Don't mind them," Leezie told Marvel. "We'll have much more fun when we take off for *you-know-where*."

"I'm proud of you," Marvel told Lee. "No one else knew how to make a fire. We didn't even know how cold we were." The warmth was nice. But it made Little Marvel feel like changing clothes. "I'm getting hot," she admitted.

As the evening grew darker, the bonfire flamed up higher and higher, until sparks went flying off into the night like lightning bugs, and the ice all around the fire began to melt, making a grand mess of slippery mud. Everything continued to thaw throughout the night, but no one noticed or seemed to care, as there was a great deal of feasting and singing and dancing. The King and Queen took a couple of spins and led a *do-si-do*.

When everyone tottered off to sleep that night, each and every one of them was warmed right through. They had never had such a party.

Lee wondered if she should go back to the sleigh to sleep that night, but then she thought to ask Marvel, "Can I sleep with

you in your stall? All of this melting is making things wet, and when I get damp, I get chilly. Maybe Beanie could join us. He looks like he might make a pretty good pillow."

Beanie looked up and yapped once, as he didn't like to be called things like pudgy pillow or burnt potato, but at the same time he liked the nice warm stable and hoped to get his little round belly rubbed.

Unbeknownst to most of the animals, Northern Joya was entering a state of transformation. A trickling river was gradually forming from the melting ice. Luckily the stable was on high ground at the back of the Palace and the stalls were still standing and the bedding dry.

54

Lee and the little pink pony and pug all cuddled up in the straw together. The hair of the girl blended in with the mane of Little Marvel. Lee threw her arms around the warm pink pony, and kissed her friend goodnight while putting her head on the chubby pug's belly.

He gave out a little snort and said, "I hope you're not a restless sleeper, 'cause your hair feels rather tickly."

But Lee was already asleep, resting happily in the dry mound of hay.

Everyone in the kingdom slept well that night, even the smitten sisters, who had been hanging around the royal sleigh, admiring the Lippizans black leather harnesses, which seemed so terribly masculine. The sisters finally fell asleep on their feet, leaning against the big white fellows. The King and Queen had actually dozed off right on their thrones, which had melted down to sloppy, slushy mounds, while the little Snowdrops drooped around them faithfully.

"Oh my," Marvel said the next morning, seeing how the Snowdrops had slumped. "It must have gotten too warm for them."

One little white flower raised her head and told the youngest pink pony, "We don't really mind. It's what we've always wanted. Spring is coming. Look at the fields!" Then the Snowdrop succumbed right before Little Marvel's eyes, and floated away on the gathering river.

Marvel was having trouble getting around. Skates were fine for ice, but not so good on mud and fields of matted grass. Little Marvel had always skated around so easily before, but now she felt wobbly, the awkward way she sometimes felt walking on the wooden floor of the stable.

"Do you want me to unlace your skates for you?" Lee asked.

Marvel had never heard of such a thing, for it seemed that her skates were part of her body, and she worried about what they would find underneath.

The knots of the skates were not easily undone, and the skates themselves had to be pried off. With the help of Garbonzo and Beanie, the front skates finally gave way and the two dogs, big and little, went tumbling backwards with a tremendous (and not so tremendous) *SPLASHsplash*.

Then there, in all their glory, were a set of pure golden hooves. Remarkable! They sparkled in the sun.

Beanie ran up and gave them a whiff. "Not too bad. They smell metallic!"

"I didn't even shine them or anything," Marvel said.

"They must be natural," Lee agreed.

"Do *you* have golden feet?" Marvel asked Lee.

She only laughed, and said, "My feet are not like yours. I have toes. They're pink, and they wiggle."

"Let's see, let's see," Beanie pounced around, until Lee unlaced her boots and pulled them off. There they were—her small pink toes, wiggling in the air.

"Whew!" the pug sniffed. "They smell like..."

"Play dough!" Bonzo barked.

"Yes, that's *it*. Exactly!" the pug dog yapped. Lee didn't mind them making fun of her feet. At least she didn't have frostbite.

Marvel was walking very oddly, picking up each foot as if it weighed very little, as if it might fly away on its own. It took a while before the youngest pink pony got the hang of walking on these new golden hooves— which soon got a bit scuffed up and muddy, which made Marvel feel more at ease. Little Marvel was much more interested in cantering about than in keeping things neat and clean. She still had this terrible urge to roll in the mud, but she didn't think anyone would appreciate that, so she held back and simply trotted in a circle.

"Do you think I might ride you sometime?" Lee asked, for she knew in her world, people rode horses.

Marvel didn't know what that meant.

"I mean, up on top of your back. On earth people use bridles and saddles."

"So that's what those leather buckets are for!" Beanie exclaimed.

They all rushed to the stable and found some saddle-buckets hanging up on racks. One of them was smaller than the others, and when they had washed it and waxed it and polished it up, it was a honey-golden color. It looked quite smart on Marvel's back, though when they tightened the girth, she had to buck a little, just to get used to the feel of the thing.

It felt even odder to have someone up on top of one's back, but it was also fun to have company. "Just please don't squeeze or kick," Marvel warned, "or I might take off by accident—I'm used to going very fast."

But now Marvel tried to take it easy. With Leezie holding onto her golden mane, they began to move forward at a pretty little walk, out to the far reaches of the melting ice fields, following the river that was heading southward as everything melted beneath Marvel's hot little hooves.

"You are so smooth!" Lee exclaimed, as Marvel extended her graceful walk and floated along without any bouncing.

On returning to the sloppy lump of what had once been the Ice Palace, they heard the white doves cooing in unison— *"What will this melting water do? To me, to you. Is Joya through?"*

Marvel had a few questions of her own—where was this river headed? Where would it lead if they followed it down?

Brilliance concluded that it was probably moving toward Southern Joya, and if the melting continued in this fashion, there could possibly be a deluge.

"What's a *day-looge*?" asked Beanie, perplexed as usual, thinking it might be a sled or toboggan.

"A flood!" cried Garbonzo. "A state of emergency," he added for good measure.

Beanie barked with a kind of snort, for he *really* liked the smell of all this mud. He liked digging it, flinging it, hopping around in it. *Snort-snort.*

"Goodness!" Luster scolded him, right there in front of the largest Lippizan. "We are going to have to call you Pug-Pig."

"I don't care," whined the muddy little dog. "Go ahead and call me. Some people aren't afraid of getting dirty. And some are far too clean for this world." He stuck his snubbed face up in the air and briskly scampered away, muddy paws and all.

"Do you think the river might lead to the Treasure House?" Lee asked the Queen in private council.

"Most likely," responded the giddy Queen. "*Every route must take you there. Isn't that nice? Isn't that fair?*"

Lee was encouraged, and took her scarf from around her neck, for it was no longer as cold as it had been the night before. Taking the edge of it, she wiped the mud from Marvel's nose. Then polished up all four golden hooves, just to see them shine. "They look like fourteen carats."

The youngest pink pony had heard about carrots, how delicious they were. *Munch-crunch.*

"Maybe we'll discover carrots growing on the south side," Lee conjectured. "Maybe we'll find the Treasure House, and I'll be able to take you home."

Lee no longer thought that she was dead, but she was worried about her mother and their baby. She even worried about her brother, too. She remembered riding in the backseat with him, hearing the sound of beer bottles under the front seat of the car. Their father had been drinking. She hated him when he was stupid like that. But no one could stop him. If they said a word, he would only get mad.

"He doesn't know what he's doing," their mother explained. But that seemed like a poor excuse. Where was her family now? She didn't think that they were in Joya, but back on earth, maybe suffering. She had to get home and find out. Only Marvel could help her now.

They agreed that together they would go as soon as possible, but that they would not tell anyone, especially the other two pink ponies.

Setting Out

Now that Leezie had thawed, she was feeling much more like herself, and ready to go home. Still longing for the comforts of her own warm bed—her nice soft quilt and feather pillow, her dear stuffed animals and her mother's food—how she longed for gravy and mashed potatoes!

Leezie had concluded that while she was not dead, she really wanted to be alive. She had to find her baby sister. Every once in a while she could hear the baby crying, but the cries seemed so far away. Sometimes she wondered if she was just dreaming. But then she'd pinch herself, and see that she was awake.

"You know I'm actually glad I came here," Lee told Marvel, "but I'd never last on this food. You might be able to survive on frozen food, but I can't."

"What do *you* like to eat?" Marvel asked, for she was used

to a diet of brittle feed, broken off from semi-frozen cubes in hard grey chunks.

"Oh, popcorn and pizza, potatoes and peas, but especially peanut butter cracker sandwiches."

"Does all your food begin with a P?"

"No, not all. I also like fruit, and not just pears, papayas and pineapples. Have you ever heard of apples?"

Marvel had to shake her head, no.

"Well, usually horses love apples. They come in red or green and even yellow. I bet they have them on the warm side of Joya. What do you think? Are you ready to go?"

Because it was still quite dark out, Marvel thought that perhaps they should wait until morning when they could ask the Queen's permission.

Lee didn't like abandoning ship without a proper thank you. The King and Queen had been exceptionally nice to her, plucking her out of that snowbank and feeding her the best they could, but sometimes when you ask permission, you risk being told *No, not yet*, or, even worse—*Maybe someday*.

"Sometimes, its best not to ask," Lee decided. "We could get stuck here forever."

"Stuck in the mud," Marvel added.

"Maybe I could write them a note."

"Oh, I'm sure they'd love a note, especially if it rhymed. Can you write it out like a poem?"

So Lee found a charred piece of charcoal left over from the fire, and composed this verse:

Dearest King and Dearest Queen,
I hope this isn't rude or mean.
I want to give my special thanks
for saving me from that cold snowbank.
You have really taken excellent care
and I was grateful for being here,
but I still miss my family lots,
so keep me in your loving thoughts.
Remember, please, as you said—
I might get home to my own warm bed
if I can find the Treasure House.
I hope you don't think I'm a louse.
Thanks again for everything.
With a ding and a dong and
a ding-a-long-ling!

Your faithful friend,
Lee Rumsey

Marvel proofed the poem and pronounced it, "Perfect! They'll love it. The Queen will probably set it to music, and lead a marching band—*Ta-ta!*" Marvel pounded both hooves on the melting snow, throwing up a spray of slush. "Can I put my hoofprint on it too?"

"Of course," Lee responded, holding the paper down for Marvel so that it could be imprinted with a solid hoof mark.

Together they raced to post it on a hook in the tack room,

and then they tiptoed ever so quietly out into the night, out under the brilliant stars. No one else was awake, but the moon was setting and the sun would soon rise and they wanted to be on their way before all of Northern Joya was up and about.

"We just need enough light to see where we're going," Lee acknowledged, as they followed the river downhill.

"Go with the flow," Marvel neighed.

Marvel was used to Lee riding now. The little pink pony's gaits had gotten even smoother and faster as she extended that pretty little walk into a kind of run—so smooth that it hardly felt like riding at all, but more like floating along on a soft, creamy carpet.

Marvel had a very steady nature, even when her head

bobbed up and down. Lee didn't have to worry about shying or bolting, plus, she knew that Marvel had a very good heart.

The youngest pink pony loved an adventure, but as they set out, Marvel had to confess that it was the first time in her entire life that she had actually entered the Great Unknown.

Without skates, Marvel had to watch her footing now, looking out for sinkholes and jagged rocks, hidden pools and obstacles. Plus, they had to make sure their supply basket didn't get stuck, for it was filled with leftovers, as well as a big chunk of thawing horse hay, and a few other dire necessities.

Lee assured Little Marvel that they would probably find green grass as soon as they got to a warmer climate, and that Marvel would find it delicious. Plus, there was the promise of apples and carrots and who knows what else. Maybe even a cup of hot chocolate!

They had been riding alone for quite some time, accompanied only by the sound of the river, (which seemed to be growing louder and louder,) when Lee admitted, "I'm so glad we're in this adventure together. I could never do this alone."

"Me either," Marvel admitted. "I guess it takes two to roam."

"So far away from home," Lee added, suddenly thinking of her mother. She asked her new friend where *her* mother was.

"I didn't ever have a mother, I don't think," Marvel said. "I was born from a tall pink hollyhock. I guess you could say that my two older sisters have been like mothers."

Hardly, Lee thought. "You should come home with me and

meet a real mother. I know she'd like you *very* much. You could live in our yard, and we'd build you a shelter. We could even ride in the park."

Lee explained that a park was a beautiful place with big trees and paths and a pond for toy boats, and that the playground had teeter-totters and jungle gyms. "It's so much fun. There are lots of kids, and there is even an ice-skating rink in the winter! You would be the champion, that's for sure!"

Marvel liked the sound of an ice-skating rink, but all of Northern Joya was like an endless rink, at least until it started to melt. Joya was also like a great, wild park, without any boundaries or fences. Marvel was not really keen on being kept in a yard. That sounded a bit confining, but she didn't say so, for fear of hurting Leezie's feelings.

The creek they were following had quickly turned into a turbulent stream with muddy banks that were often slippery. And then when they turned a corner, the stream met another faster river. Joining forces, the gushing water became torrential!

"I've never seen so much water in my entire life," Marvel pawed the riverbank. Little Marvel was used to slowly dripping icicles, not wild white water of this sort.

"Oh, someday I'll take you to the ocean, and we can run on the beach. Wouldn't that be fun? But this river is definitely leading us onward. It's getting warmer every minute."

Marvel agreed. "It's making me hot!" It was true. Marvel was lathering up from all the exertion. "Maybe we should take a break," Lee suggested, spotting a ledge that seemed nice and firm. They both climbed up over a pile of rocks to rest there on the smooth, dry ledge.

Marvel even sampled some odd bits of old grass that had been buried under the winter snow, nodding up and down.

Lee slipped off the golden saddle and found that Marvel was sweating profusely. "Let me brush you," she suggested. "It will help cool you off."

She found a curry comb in the laundry basket and began to brush Marvel's shaggy pink coat, but as Lee worked,

the strangest thing happened—huge hunks of hair fell out in her hands.

"Yikes! You seem to be molting," Lee cried. She didn't realize that shedding is what happens to horses after winter is over and springtime arrives. Yes, horses do lose their old woolly coats, but what was most amazing now, was that as Marvel's winter pink fell out, a purple satin coat lay underneath. It was incredibly beautiful!

"My Gosh," Lee cried. "Just look at you!"

But Marvel couldn't see what Leezie saw, because there were no ice mirrors in this melting, muddy, middle ground. She didn't dare look at her reflection in the river for fear of falling in and getting swept away.

"Did you know you had a different outfit underneath the pink one? You're as purple and pretty as a plum! You are going to be so, so beautiful, much better than your silly sisters."

Marvel seemed to like this shedding business, getting rid of that tiresome old pink fluff, enjoying the feel of the brush along her back and neck and down her strong little legs. Purple was more like it! She felt like she was becoming more and more marvelous with every stroke!

"You still have three pink polka dots on your rump," Lee rubbed Marvel's rear in small firm circles. Marvel grew sleeker and shinier as Lee continued to brush. The more purple she became, the more her mane and tail and hooves appeared to be a brighter and shinier gold.

Without thinking, Lee remembered a silly rhyme her mother

used to say: *I've never seen a purple cow, I never hope to see one. But I can tell you this right now, I'd rather see than be one.*

Marvel repeated the rhyme to herself, then hung her head. "Why wouldn't you want to *be* one? Don't you like purple?"

"Of course I do," Lee answered. "It's just a nonsense rhyme." But then Lee realized that she had hurt Little Marvel's feelings, and so she added, "Anyone would want to be a beautiful purple like you. You are absolutely glistening!"

This made Marvel feel better. "I never felt like I was much of a pink pony. I never fit in with my sisters. Take those Lippizans for instance. UGH."

"You do seem different. Do you feel different, too?"

Marvel had to admit that yes, she did. "This color suits me."

"I was never much of a pink person myself. I always preferred blue, which is supposed to be a boy's color, but we should be able to pick any color we want."

"Yes," Marvel responded, "And I choose YOU!"

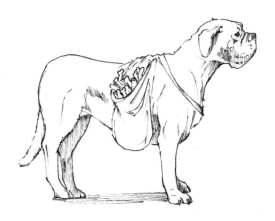

Come Along Lately

Meanwhile, dawn had arrived in Northern Joya. The birds had awakened and the last of the Snowdrops stretched up to greet the morning sun. Though they had lost their little white bonnets, they now stood taller and straighter and greener, with slender grassy leaves.

Luster and Brince went to check on their tack, for they wanted to look especially nice for their two big consorts, the powerful, white Lippizans, and what did they find on the hook of the tack room—the astonishing handwritten, hoofprinted message from Marvel and Lee Rumsey.

"This isn't even good hoofmanship," Luster snorted, in her most refined manner.

Brilliance read the note over twice. She could hardly believe her eyes. It was clear that their youngest *subling* had run off with that ghastly child! This was hard to comprehend, but Brince, being the smart one, knew it was true.

The two pink sisters let out an alarm-neigh that woke the rest of the Kingdom.

Bonzo and Beanie came bounding up, for even when half-asleep, they were still on guard and alert to any warning signal. "What's Up, WHAT'S UP?" they barked in unison.

The King and Queen came scuttling into the stable to investigate the source of all the commotion, dragging along their damp and muddy robes. "Hear, hear," cried the King. "What's this all about? I believe it is time for breakfast."

"Marvel and Leezie are gone!" Brince neighed. "I should have known that something like this would happen. I should have been more alert."

"We must, we must, we *must*," barked Bonzo, unable to finish his sentence.

"Follow them or BUST!" barked the pug.

"*We must, we must, we must develop our trust,*" sang the Queen, marching around in a circle.

The King pulled her up short by saying, "This is quite serious, My Dear."

"Since when have we become serious?"

"As of right now," affirmed the King. "Look around you—look at the state of things. Everything's melting beneath our feet! Look at that rivulet—it's become a river. Those two could get swept away!"

"We must go after them," Bonzo declared.

"We can pull the sleigh," the largest Lippizan whinnied.

Hearing this, Luster looked distraught. Wouldn't the

runners get stuck in the mud? "You had better stay here with us," she exclaimed.

Bonzo continued to read the note upwards and downwards, backwards and forwards, front to back and back to front. It said the same thing in each case, but it did look different upside down.

"Don't hold a horseshoe upside down," barked Beanie, "or all the good luck will drain out!"

"I imagine they are headed for the Treasure House," the Queen said. "We should gather a grand parade and go!"

"But first we must have our breakfast." The King was feeling a little bit grumpy.

"We'll lead the reconnaissance mission," cried Bonzo.

"We shall lead the way," added Beanie. "And we don't need a royal sleigh, either," sneering a bit at the huge white Lippizans who had given in so easily.

"You go," sang the jolly Queen, "and we'll follow."

"*Follow, follow, follow,*" chimed the last of the Snowdrops.

"All in due time," added the King. "After a little split toast stuffed with marmalade."

Luster checked on the response of her big white Lippizan, who shook his head up and down in agreement. The Lippizans were flattered by the pink ponies' attention, and they weren't too eager to leave these blushing beauties behind. Neither Luster nor Brince was very adventurous. They were happy to

stay put, taking care of the stable and the melting remains of the Ice Kingdom, though the slush did make a mess of things, splattering their once perfect, pale pink coats. They whisked it away for each other, and tried to keep as polished and pretty as possible.

"I want to go NOW," Bonzo announced, looking to the King for permission.

"You don't need a *Neigh* or a *Yeah* from me, anymore. We melted our crowns, don't forget. You animals have to listen to your own hearts now. Obey your own inner instincts."

"*On the inside!*" Beanie cheered. But then he thought better and asked the Queen, "Can we ask the Pink Cloud what to do? I'll close my eyes and just think of Her."

"Surely," the Queen encouraged. "But be off now, my darling poopy dogs! We'll meet up with you one of these days."

With this encouragement Bonzo and Beanie packed biscuits and bones and headed out, following the quickly dissolving hoofmarks which were being washed away by the rising water.

Both dogs had excellent noses (thirty times more powerful than humans, you know), and they could smell their friend Marvel from miles away—though the smell appeared to be changing from sweet cotton candy to something more tart. They tried not to get confused.

"The girl still smells like play dough, don't you think?" Beanie barked.

Bonzo shrugged. "Or yesterday's french fries, hold the ketchup. I sure hope this river doesn't outrun us!"

At times they lost sight of Marvel's hoofprints, because the pony had traversed the stream here and there, to avoid a fallen log or a very large boulder. But finally the dogs came upon a campsite, where the travelers had probably eaten some leftovers, and there was also a puff of pink pony clothes in a great big pile. Beanie leapt on the heap, kicking the fluff up into the air.

"Don't litter," Garbonzo reprimanded the pug. "You're getting that stuff all over the place."

"*But shedding makes good bedding*," cried Beanie. "Where do you think this all came from?"

"It smells like Marvel to me."

"It does!" and with one tremendous inhalation, little Beanie, who was rather exhausted from the first leg of their trip—since he had to walk twice as fast as the big dog—dropped himself into the soft pink pile and fell instantly asleep.

Bonzo walked around in circles before he too collapsed with a groan, nudging the pug to keep him from snoring. "*Hush your mush*," Bonzo growled in his grumpy, affectionate way.

The pug responded with a short *snort-snort*. He was dreaming of rushing water, twitching and whimpering in his sleep, trying to escape from something.

When they woke from their nap, it was the next day and the river was truly roaring. They could barely hear each other bark over the tumult.

"*Lousy NOISE*," Beanie screamed at the top of his lungs,

yapping at the rushing water, "*is bad for boys*!" He then darted
out to grab a nice smooth stick from the bank, as if to save it
from extinction. "Will you throw it? Will you toss it for me?" the
little pug pranced. He was used to having fun when he was out
for a walk.

"Bothersome dog," grumbled Garbonzo. But he gave in and
tossed the stick a few times, before telling Beanie to hop up onto
a rock and get on his back. "We've got to get going, and you
might as well ride."

Beanie hopped right onto the mastiff's back, gripping the stick in his teeth as if it were his most precious possession.

"It's nice to have something to chew on," Beanie explained, "to help pass the time of day."

"Don't talk with your mouth full," Garbonzo scolded, "or you'll lose your balance. Goodness, some people do all the work, and others are just along for the ride."

"Would you rather I carry *you*?" queried the saucy little pug.

"Yeah, *right*," Garbonzo replied. "Hang on," he shouted over his shoulder, before making a leap toward the far side—but instead of crossing all the way over, the big dog's feet slipped on the muddy bank and the two of them went sliding into the rushing river. Suddenly they were paddling madly downstream—it was all they could do to keep their heads above water. Luckily, both dogs were pretty good swimmers, but Beanie had to drop his precious stick, and almost sank when he tried to retrieve it.

"Leave that thing and *swim*," barked Bonzo, "Go with the Flow-oh-NO!" he disappeared over a river rock, where the water pounded. Then he popped back up, a ways downstream, gasping for air.

Just then Lee happened to look up and saw the two dogs paddling furiously past them. "Look! It's Bonzo and Beanie! Catch them, Marvel, HURRY," she cried.

Marvel rushed to the river's edge and plunged in, never thinking about herself or worrying about the danger—she only wanted to rescue their friends.

Marvel swam up beside the larger dog and whinnied—"Take hold of my mane!"

Garbanzo growled, not recognizing the true colors of this plum-colored pony. "It's not like I have hands," the big dog snapped.

"Use your jaws. It won't hurt me!"

And so he did, while Beanie grabbed onto the big dog's ruff and they were both pulled out of the torrent to shore.

All three of them lay there in the mud trying to catch their collective breath (much harder than catching a ball or a stick), but when they could all breathe again, they took a good look at each other, and started to laugh, "It's you!"

"Who me?"

"Yes YOU!"

"Couldn't be!"

"Then who?"

They laughed so hard they almost cried, so gloriously happy to be out of that freezing water, safe on good, dry land.

Lee came running up to the dogs and gave each of them a big hug. They recognized her immediately, but they were still confused, as if their heads were stuck in a whirlpool and they were rather dizzy.

"Who's the purple pony?" Beanie asked.

"Aren't you going to introduce us?" added Garbonzo. "And what have you done with our friend?"

"It's Me!" Marvel announced, looking up from the bright green grass. "*Friends friends, til the end?*"

Both dogs gazed at each other, stunned, and then back to the purple pony, taking a sniff. "A little bit different from what I remember," said Garbonzo.

"But more or less, less or more," pronounced Beanie. "I guess it's just the change of clothes, but you smell rather fruity."

Marvel leaned down and gave the pug a nudge.

"Let me look at your hoofprint," demanded the mastiff.

Marvel stamped her golden hoof in the dirt, and both dogs read it backwards and forwards and upside down. They admitted that it was the exact same signature.

"I always thought because my sisters and I came from the same pink hollyhock, that we would remain the same, but I actually like being different."

"And quite a fine color you are," nodded the pug, tilting his head this way, then that. "Royalty often wears purple."

"I must say I was pretty frightened back there," Garbonzo admitted. "I thought we were going to drown. Thanks for saving our lives."

"Yeah, thanks for saving a life that's hardly even worth living," added the pug. "I've never been so hungry in my entire life. Do you have any nourishment?"

"We don't have much left in our basket," Lee admitted, "but look over there." She pointed away from the river and through the forest, where they saw an open meadow beyond. "Maybe we can find some berry bushes or apple trees."

"Or a tasty biscuit and a juicy bone!"

The dogs kept inspecting their old friend Marvel who looked

so new and different all dressed up in purple, but there was the same wild mane and golden tail and the same nice disposition.

"I think you've grown some," the pug decided. "We can't call you *little* anymore."

"What *are* we supposed to call you now?" Garbonzo asked.

"How about—Marvel the Marvelous," Lee suggested.

And so that was the end (and the beginning) of that.

What They
Found Underground

*B*ounding ahead of everyone, yipping and yapping, the chubby little pug thought he saw a bone tree in the distance.

The mastiff barked, "Wait up!" for he felt it was probably some sort of mirage, set there to fool them, "To, To, TO— *Trap Us!*" he barked as he fell head over heels into a very deep hole, where the scrambling, plummeting pug had just disappeared into utter darkness.

Descending echoes floated up from the deep, dark shaft as Marvel and Lee stopped short of the edge. Together they both heard the double *thudTHUD* of the two dogs landing one on top of the other—unfortunately the big dog on top of the small. Then their moans and groans rose from the bottom in a kind of delirious, doggie duet. *"Ow Wow—Ugh my Mug."*

"I can't see a thing," Lee whispered, peering down into the dreadful hole. "Are you ok? Ok? OK?" she shouted.

"Certainly *not! Not! NOT!*" barked the mastiff.

"We've got to go *down, Down, DOWN*, and help them," Marvel exclaimed.

"But *how How HOW?* How can we help them, if they're at the bottom of some mineshaft? How will we ever get down there*?*"

The deep hole gave Leezie a creepy feeling, for there was this terrible sucking wind, and she thought if she went all the way down, it might suck her soul right up.

But Marvel was not to be deterred. "There must be an exit. Every entrance has an exit hole, and whoever built this tunnel must have had some plan."

Maybe it wasn't a very nice plan, Leezie thought. Maybe it was a way of trapping things. "How will we ever get down there without hurting ourselves?" She knew she was being a coward, but Marvel nudged her out of it.

"Don't forget, you're with me. *No dog left behind!*"

"I'm just saying that maybe there might be a safer way to help them than plunging headlong down some dreadful mine shaft. Maybe we could find a rope or vine to pull them out."

But Marvel had another idea. She thought if she spread herself out, she could reach either side of the shaft, and then they could descend hoof-by-hoof.

Lee really did not care for deep, dark places, especially when they threatened to suck her up, and she almost suggested that perhaps Marvel might go down alone, that the purple pony would have greater success without her additional weight, but Marvel didn't want to leave Lee behind. Who knew what was lurking about up there in the woods. No, Lee had better mount up.

As they entered the deep dark mine shaft, descending deeper and deeper into oblivion, Lee noted that Marvel's mane and hooves became more and more luminous—a radiant gold, which brightened their descent with a glowing light.

As they got closer to the bottom, she could easily see Garbonzo and Beanie lying in a furry heap. But they were whimpering and moaning in such an odd embrace that she could barely tell who was who.

The pug dog had apparently broken a bone in his foot and would have to be carried. "I think it's my baby toe," he complained. "It's always something, I tell you."

"You're lucky that Bonzo can carry you," Lee responded. She couldn't stop herself from saying—"Guess who got us into this mess?"

"Who?" the pug responded with a snort of self-pity. Then he remembered that he had been the first to fall. "Well, I couldn't help it. I thought I saw a bone tree. You can't blame me for trying, when I've been SO very hungry all night and day, and now I am starving *and* broken to pieces. I think I am going to be in a very foul mood, unless people start being nice to me." The pug began to scold them all, as if this mess was somebody else's fault.

"Some people can never take responsibility for their actions," the mastiff complained. "You should look where you're going once in a while, and not be in such a rush."

"You're not the boss of me!" the pug barked back, insolent as ever.

"Oh, hush your mush," said Garbonzo. "You're not the only one who's sore. At least you broke my fall. You are rather plump and a fairly good cushion."

"*Hmpf*," the pug retorted.

88

"Some people always have to have the last word."

"Word!" barked the pug.

Garbonzo let it drop, like a bone that had had all the life chewed out of it.

"We're not at the bottom of this, exactly," Marvel beamed the light from her lustrous forelock—"Can you see how this tunnel turns and then runs along the flat?"

"I wonder where it goes?" Garbonzo worried. "Probably nowhere very nice. What is that sucking sound?"

At least Bonzo heard it too, Lee thought. She felt it tugging at her, as if it wanted to pull her right out of her boots. It was a kind of empty whistling sound—sucking in, rather than blowing out.

"Tunnels always go somewhere," Marvel said with a leader's assurance.

"I think I'd rather go back up," Lee complained, and Beanie agreed, but Marvel had already started nosing town the tunnel and the rest were forced to follow, because the purple pony was the only one with any light and no one wanted to be left in the darkness without possibility of escape.

The further they went, the stronger the sound became. Moisture was dripping from the ceiling, and the path became very slick. Lee would surely have turned around if she hadn't been holding onto Marvel's golden tail, which at least gave her some assurance.

"What's that?" whimpered Beanie. Everybody stopped, and stood there listening. Yes, in the distance, they could hear a high, shrill sound, and then they felt a thundering, rattling vibration, as if a miniature battalion was barreling right toward them.

"Good grief," said Bonzo. "*Rats.*"

"What's next?" demanded Beanie with a *snort, snort-snort.* "It's always something, I tell you."

"Leap to the side!" Marvel instructed, but Lee felt paralyzed. The squealing noise grew louder and louder, more high-pitched, and Lee couldn't move, as if stuck in a very bad dream.

Finally, as the rats rounded the corner, she forced herself to lurch, but instead of leaping to the side, she slipped in the mud and went down, groping and sliding on the greasy mud as a squealing stream of rats raced over her with their nasty, frantic little claws.

She flailed her arms and legs in a futile effort to keep them off, and one ran up her pants leg! She yelled and screamed and shook herself wildly, jumping up and down, shaking her pants until the animal found its way back out and scurried after the others. *UGH!*

Lee buried her face in Marvel's mane as a shudder of horror swept through her. There was nothing that Marvel could say or do to make her feel any better.

"Nasty, *nasty,*" the pug said for emphasis. "I'm glad it didn't happen to me."

"At least it didn't bite you," offered Bonzo, but that was little comfort.

"I wonder what they were running from? Something must have frightened them. I've heard of rats running from a sinking ship," Marvel went, "but we can't be sinking, when we're underground."

It was at times like this that Marvel missed her sister Brilliance, who was always able to figure these things out. Lee was unable to think herself, for she couldn't get rid of the horrible feeling of the rodent's tiny claws. She shuddered and shook and had to jump up and down to shake the sensation off.

Lee put her hand out onto the tunnel wall, and felt even more repulsed, for the wall of the tunnel was slippery and slimy, as if it were a giant intestine, quivering, flesh-like. "Get me OUT of here!" Lee cried. "If we go any further, we'll probably end up in somebody's stomach!"

"Is somebody trying to eat us?" yelped the pug.

"Don't be an alarmist," Bonzo growled.

"Look who's talking!"

Marvel had already spotted a giant cave-like area up ahead. There were all sorts of disturbing noises coming from that direction.

"It sounds like indigestion," Lee said.

As they entered the cavern, the water was bubbling, steaming and seething. There was even the corpse of some little mammal and a fluttering baby bird floating along in the nasty brew.

"Can we *please* get out of here?" Lee implored.

"I second that suggestion," Beanie agreed.

But Marvel's motto was, "*Never go back!*"

"*Never go back to Hackensack,*" sang Bonzo, for he didn't relish the thought of following rats, even if they did have good instincts for self-preservation.

On the floor of the cave chamber was a smelly brown pool that seemed to smell somewhat familiar. Lee could almost name it, though she was still in a bit of a fog from her latest ordeal, and had a kind of earthly amnesia where she couldn't always come up with the name for certain things, especially familiar sensations like this one. But then it was right on the rim of her brain, and then something in her mind tipped over, for she had smelled this smell before—her father's breath. She remembered it now, a sodden *burp*, and then she almost shouted—"*BEER!*"

She remembered how her Dad had been drinking on the day of the accident. She remembered the sound of those long brown bottles under the front seat of the car. How stupid to drink when you were driving. Everybody knew that. But nobody could stop him or tell him what to do. He would just get mad.

Lee felt sick to her stomach, remembering that smell, but then another vile wave of the stuff came sloshing in, bubbling and fizzing around their ankles.

"No wonder those rats were running!" Beanie squealed. "Get me out of here before I get drunk!"

All sorts of debris was floating in the brownish ale, old bits of partially eaten flotsam and jetsam, hot dog wrappers with smears of mustard, bottle caps and baby Pampers. Beanie turned his nose up at what might have once been almost edible fare, but he was the Queen's own lapdog, and would not stoop to such unsavory, sloshed-about scraps.

Amidst all this commotion, Lee noted the sucking wind again. It pulled her forward a few steps, and her hair got in her eyes. She thought she could hear her baby sister crying way down some distant corridor. Was baby Claire being swallowed up? Lee knew that she had to find her sister, so she was eager to follow Marvel when their leader commanded the group, "Move forward." Though the tunnel seemed to get smaller and nastier the further they went, there did seem to be a pinprick of light up ahead.

If it weren't for Marvel leading the way, Lee never would have had the courage to enter the narrowing exit hole, though one of her hands was firmly wrapped around Marvel's tail. She lent her other hand to Beanie's paw while he sat on the back of Garbonzo.

"Don't squeeze," he pleaded. "I'm badly hurt."

"Our invalid," muttered Bonzo.

"Let's not fuss. We're almost out," Marvel whinnied.

Together, they all squeezed further and further along until they noticed another roaring, like the crash of an incoming wave—and suddenly a new surge of dark brown liquid came swooshing along behind them. The beer infused substance came pummeling through, picking them up and carrying them forward, spitting them out of the exit hole where they popped back out into fine fresh air with a collective—"*WHEW* and *AHHH*."

Looking at each other, they began to laugh, for all of them were covered from head to toe in slimy, greasy mud.

"Gross," said Garbonzo."

"P.U.!" said the pug.

"Add a G and you have—"

"What?" Beanie snorted, quickly turning his back on the bigger dog, for he knew how to spell the word "pug" and the smell had nothing to do with him. Beanie scooted over to the water's edge and tested it with his toe.

Lee was eager to bathe, and thought of her mother running warm tub water, handing her the slippery bar of pink soap which she shot up and down, making the water milky. How much she missed her mother sometimes!

Once the muck was washed from their faces, they could see they were in the Heart of Joya. Flowers were growing everywhere, even all over the trees, and there was a waterfall.

"Look, strawberries. Ripe ones too! And bright green grass for Marvel to munch upon."

Marvel nibbled a little, and then some more.

"Isn't there anything here for a couple of starving dogs?" asked Garbonzo, for canines didn't care much for fruit or grass.

"Do you like mushrooms?" Leezie asked. "There seem to be plenty of nice white mushrooms."

The two dogs looked at each other, and did not know. "They might be deadly poisonous," whispered the mastiff.

"What we need is a bone tree," squealed Beanie, "or, or, or... some caramel pudding!"

When the little troop came around the corner and saw the waterfall, they forgot all about food, because the Middle Kingdom of Joya was like nothing they had ever seen before. There were white doves whirling in the lavender sky, and many-colored, brilliant butterflies, yellow and orange and turquoise too, floating in the air above the falling water, which was silvery, fresh and sparkling. The water in the pool was bathtub warm—they all plunged in at the base of the waterfall and took a much needed shower.

Floating on her back, Lee watched the colorful birds wheeling overhead. They sang the most glorious songs. She also noticed that flowers were covering the banks with lush abundance. There was a wonderful perfumed scent in the air—

a bit like cherries or hyacinths—so welcome after the stench of the tunnel.

When Marvel hopped out of the water, her radiant purple coat looked like a polished plum. She danced off into a field of purple crocus and no one could see her for a minute. All they could make out was her mane and tail.

"Marvel, come back!" Lee cried. "Where are you?" She didn't want to lose her companion to a field of flowers. It made her realize how horrible it would be to lose her very best friend.

She scouted around until she found a bush of juicy blackberries, and gathered a handful to entice the horse.

Marvel finally came trotting out of the crocus field to sample the berries Lee held out, and the purple pony got sweet, dark juice all over her nose. She gave Lee a juicy smack on the cheek, leaving a purple imprint.

"Don't worry so much," Marvel whispered. "*Friends, friends til the end.*"

"To what end?" Lee questioned. She hated to think of anything ending.

Marvel's glorious new coat shone more purple than ever. She seemed to be gaining strength and tone with every step. She no longer looked like a pony, but more like a graceful, powerful horse. Surely she would help Lee find the Treasure House and get her home to her family.

Lee was still hoping that Marvel would come back home with her and live in their yard, but then, on the other hand, as

Beanie said, "I don't ever want to leave this place. It's just about absolutely perfect!"

Lee wondered if she ever left Joya, would she be able to return? Could she come back in the spring with the purple crocus and pay Marvel and her friends a visit? Her heart seemed to tug in both directions, and she felt pulled apart. She wanted to see her family, to know how they were, but this beautiful place was how she imagined a fairytale heaven, and she did not want to leave. Everything was shining with color and filled with vibrant opalites. Everything seemed so wonderfully good, intensely alive, yet peaceful too. It almost hurt her eyes, it was so pretty, and it smelled so delicious, like cherries and sugar and warm, creamy vanilla all mixed together. It was enough just to breath the air.

Marvel plunged back under the waterfall, liking the way it streamed all over her. Bonzo and Beanie dog-paddled around while Lee splashed her feet in the glistening water. It felt good to be so clean.

Finally, they all lay down on the sandy banks of the shore and dried themselves in the sun. Lee didn't want to think about the stench of that slimy soul-sucking tunnel. She wasn't about to analyze their journey or to try and make sense of what had happened to them, but she believed they were making progress, going in the right direction.

Now, at last, they all had fruit to snack on, and Marvel was gaining strength from the fresh green grass, and the mushrooms had magically melted into little cups of caramel pudding, as if mere wishing had made it so. Both dogs were lapping it up by the gallon until they suddenly fell into a very sound slumber.

"Maybe we should let them rest," Lee suggested.

"Maybe we have no choice," said Marvel. "That pudding must have contained a potion."

"Hopefully, they will sleep it off," Lee suggested. That's what her mother always used to say—that her father would have to sleep it off. He was usually better by morning.

The sand on the shore was so comfortable and warm, it was easy to relax. As the sun sank beneath the rim of the mountains, the stars began to shine. The evening air was deeply fragrant and fireflies lit up the balmy air. Lee cuddled up on Marvel's shoulder, and pulled the rippling, blond mane over her. There on the banks of this small, serene lake, they slept peacefully until dawn.

When they awoke, Marvel and Lee felt fine, but the dogs were still in a coma. "Drugged, I think," said Marvel.

"Try splashing them with water."

Marvel kicked a spray of water over them, but not even a good dousing could awaken their friends. The dogs were still breathing, twitching in their sleep as if they were being chased by something.

"*HELLOOOOO!*" Lee yelled, but nothing could wake the mastiff or the pug, not even a kiss or a tickle.

Entering the Glume

"What shall we do now?" Lee asked, knowing that Marvel had a good sense of direction, and would instinctively know which way to go.

Marvel glanced across the water to a set of stairs that went up and up at a radical angle. "What do you think? Are you game?"

"I am, if you are."

"I are, if you am," Marvel answered, and they both laughed. It was good to begin the next phase of their journey with clean bodies and light hearts even if they were still a little bit baffled.

"But what about the dogs?" Lee worried. "They're still asleep."

"We had better leave them a note."

So Lee found a stick and wrote in the sand: BE BACK LATER. Marvel put her imprint beneath it, and Leezie pressed her foot mark too. She just hoped the dogs would wake up on their own, and have enough sense to follow. The dogs did look happy enough sleeping there, but too much sleep can be as disturbing as too little. Maybe they were in some kind of coma, Lee thought.

Leezie then leapt into the saddle and Marvel began her pretty little walk around the perimeter of the lake. Lee loved this gait, where she wasn't jarred or bounced but carried along so smoothly—it was almost as if they were flying.

But Marvel was still worrying about the dogs. The steep pitch of the steps would be hard on Garbonzo, especially with Beanie on his back.

"Hold onto my mane," Marvel instructed. "This is going to be quite a climb."

Lee put all of her weight into the stirrups, and leaned forward as far as she could, gripping Marvel's golden mane, thinking—*Onward and Upward, Marvelous!*

Marvel took the marble steps briskly, one hoof at a time. It was as if the steps were placed perfectly for their ascent, but as the two of them climbed higher and higher, Marvel began struggling for breath. The further they went, the darker the sky became, as if they were entering a very dense fog. And then at the top of the staircase, they found themselves standing in a dreadful dimness.

"Where in the land of Joya are we?" Lee thought out loud. "It certainly does seem like we are *on the inside*, like the inside of some kind of storage closet." She thought she even caught a whiff of mothballs.

Marvel kept trying to catch her breath, but could only breathe with great difficulty. The entire sky had turned from a lovely lavender-blue to a grayish-brown.

"Can you see your hand?" Marvel asked.

"Not really." Lee moved her hand in front of her face. "Can you see your hooves?"

"No, not at all."

"Why don't you turn your light on?"

But when Marvel tried to brighten her forelock, it was dim too, as if this smog was capable of draining her light force.

"Strange," Marvel had to admit—"I've never seen anything like this."

In Northern Joya, even when it was freezing, there was always an abundance of light, which helped to lift the animals' spirits, but this dimness was downright depressing.

The beautiful perfumed air had also disappeared, replaced by a strong acidic smell. There was an eerie sound floating about them—like a painful snore on the inhale, with a whistling moan on the exhale. It seemed familiar. Maybe it was connected to that soul-sucking sound they had heard down in that slimy tunnel.

Feeling their way along, step by step, careful not to trip, Lee asked, "How is your footing?"

"Not good." Marvel felt strangely low in spirit, and Lee knew that was not normal.

They continued to grope their way along, Marvel shuffling forward bit by bit until she smashed her muzzle against a wall. *That hurt!*

Lee gave her friend a comforting rub on the neck, and together they crept along the wall, until they finally tumbled into a dreary, dormant garden.

The moaning and groaning got heavier and louder. They didn't know where they were, but there seemed to be nowhere else to go.

The dark cloud obscured almost everything now, except for what they could see directly beneath them, between their hooves and feet. Yes, the flowers were all sound asleep here, or perhaps they had wilted out of despair. There was certainly a heavy feeling pressing down, as if life had turned very miserable indeed.

"This seems the opposite of Joya," Lee cried. She could feel a terrible aching in her chest, and it made her awfully homesick. She was afraid she might burst into tears, sobs that would be

hard to explain, even to Marvel. She tried to hide her feelings, but Marvel sensed Lee's sadness.

"Are you feeling bad?" Marvel nudged her friend.

"Yeah," Lee admitted. "I'm feeling a little bit weepy." It was at that moment that Lee realized that Marvel never showed sadness. Maybe her friend didn't know what true sadness was. Lee put a hand on Marvel's sleek purple shoulder, and asked, "Don't *you* ever cry?"

Lee thought she could feel Marvel wince.

"I don't think horses do that."

Lee thought her friend was simply not capable of tears. Maybe horses didn't feel things the same way humans did. It made both of them feel rather glum. They were so close and yet so different.

"I'm sorry," Lee continued. "I just feel like all of our struggles have been for naught, and now I've dragged you into this terrible mess and I'll probably never get home."

A rusty watering can had fallen at the edge of the path next to an old decrepit wagon. "That's how I feel," Lee pointed, "useless." The snoring and whistling seemed to get louder and louder, and it gave her the creeps.

Finally, at the edge of a dried up pit, Marvel had to admit, "We're lost."

What did that mean? For they had been exploring new territory throughout their entire journey. Neither of them had really known where they were going once they had left the realm of the north, so how could they be any more lost right now than they had been in that muddy tunnel, or by the side of the lake, for that matter?

Lee tried to muster some optimism. "You just have to put one hoof in front of the other. Step by step, we'll get there."

"I guess so," Marvel nodded, but her head was hanging unusually low.

Marvel was still thinking about Lee's comment, and wondering if she were capable of tears. Was she lacking something essential? She knew she wasn't a human being, but did that make her any less sensitive?

"Maybe horses don't make good friends," Marvel said, "if they can't even cry like humans."

"You make a wonderful friend. I'm sure you do things that I can't do, like whisk flies away with your tail."

"Big deal." That didn't seem like much of an accomplishment. Marvel kept looking down at her golden hooves, thinking they were awfully dull.

Finally Marvel had the glimmer of an idea. In the past, she had called on the Pink Cloud of Perfection, who always had an excellent suggestion. "But I wonder if I'll be able to hear what She says, now that I'm no longer pink. Maybe She won't recognize me anymore."

"You still have those three pink spots on your rump," Lee reminded her friend.

"I guess," Marvel answered, morosely.

"Do you think you'll be able to hear anything over this terrible drone?"

"I wonder if She'll even come *near* all this GLOOM."

At that moment, a little Violet flower raised her pathetic wee head and whispered, "That's the word alright. We're oppressed by Spigot-Von-Glume. I hope you can help us before we expire. We need water and light, and we're awfully tired."

Lee put her head close to the little purple-faced flower. "What did you say? What was that?"

"*Spigot-von-Glume*," the Violet whispered, before seeming to collapse on her stem.

It was almost as if Lee could taste the dark rotten fog that surrounded them, and it tasted, or smelled like... "Dog farts!"

"Excuse *Me*?" a familiar voice piped up. It was Beanie speaking. And there was Garbonzo—two shapes appearing out of the dimness.

Lee had to laugh with delight. The little pug dog was dragging a very large sack of some sort.

"Please don't compare me to this stinky fog, or whatever the heck it is. P! U!"

"Add a G and you have— ?"

"What? Well, it certainly wasn't me!"

Lee was so happy to see the dogs, she threw her arms around Bonzo's neck, and gave Beanie a great big kiss.

"Don't slobber," Beanie twirled away, and Marvel's light seemed to pulse for a moment, illuminating their old traveling companions.

"Why did you leave us?" Garbonzo complained. "That made us *very* anxious."

"You abandoned us while we slept!" shrieked Beanie.

"I'm sorry," Marvel nudged both dogs in turn. "We just couldn't wake you, so we thought we'd get a little hoof start."

"Yeah, *right*," said Garbonzo.

"Meanies!" yapped the pug. "Somebody must have drugged us, and then all those terrible steps! And now this gloom. It's always something, I tell you."

"What do you have there?" Lee asked the pug, giving the bag a little shove with her foot.

Beanie yanked it away from her, saying, "My bone bag."

Garbonzo gave them another clue. "Gold, pure gold. Not

great for chewing, but maybe good for something, somehow, sometimes, someday." Then he went on to ask—"Marvel, are you going to get us out of this place? We're counting on you."

And the pug chimed in, *"One-two, one-two—What will we do? Please save us from this awful stew!"*

"Marvel ain't the Boss of *you*, is she?" Bonzo reminded the pug, who didn't like having his own words rearranged and tossed back at him, so he gave the bigger dog a bang with the bone bag.

"That hurts," Bonzo barked. Everyone was getting on each other's nerves.

But then Lee noticed that Marvel was standing absolutely still, communing with the golden Pink Cloud of Perfection. All of a sudden they could hear a melodic rumble approaching from far above the persistent snoring-droning sound of the depressing Spigot-Von-Glume.

Spigot Speaks

"*I* feel like I'm withering up," Beanie complained, collapsing onto his haunches.

"I'm the one that's been carrying *you*," said Bonzo. "So why don't you quit your complaining."

"You don't have to be so *mean*!"

"I'm not, you little poop head."

"Stop it, both of you," Lee told the dogs. "That's not helping us one bit. In fact, I think that is just what this Spigot-Von-Glume wants—to suck up all our happiness, and leave us feeling nasty and mean."

"Yeah, mad and bad," Bonzo added.

"And a teeny bit sad," Beanie continued this depressing train of thought.

But Marvel was looking up and Up and UP. "Hush, and let me listen." A voice that made all of them stand perfectly still. Marvel wobbled a bit, trying to concentrate.

Maybe they were breathing in poisonous fumes. Lee gripped her stomach, feeling nauseous, and Beanie whispered, "I feel rotten."

"Keep picturing the Pink," Marvel instructed, neighing softly—"There She IS! Can you feel it?"

"I smell Her coming," barked the pug. It was like fresh, springtime air, pure, delicious!

And yes, Lee thought she could hear the sound of little silver chimes approaching, and then it sounded more and more

like bells at midday, gonging and ringing, so that the snoring and droning and blowing sounds made by the dreadful Spigot-Von-Glume were almost driven away.

As if out of nowhere, the Pink Cloud whispered, *Why don't you speak to the Darkness. Listen to it, and do so with Kindness.*

Marvel wrestled with this message in her own confused mind, trying to understand. She then summoned up all of her courage and addressed the Glume—"Hello out there. How are you?"

There was nothing but a stunned silence for a very long while, but the moaning seemed to pause, as if it had heard and was astonished at being addressed at all.

"I was wondering how you feel?" Marvel continued.

A cold whistling wind preceded the answer, and there was a sudden chill as it spoke. "I am *verrrrrrrry lowwwwwnely.*"

There was silence then, and it almost seemed as if this gloomy being was silently sobbing all by itself, like somebody lost under a heavy blanket.

Leezie knew what it felt like to be lost and alone—it was almost more painful when you couldn't let your grief show, but had to stuff it away somewhere and live with it half-hidden.

"*I am also alllllllllllways verrrrrrrry hunnnnnngry,*" it went on, "*and neverrrrrrrrrrrrrrrr everrrrrrrrrrrrrrrr satisfied.*"

The long extended *rrrr* sound made it seem as if this being was shivering from the cold inside itself.

"*Do you have annnnnnnnything to eat? I like sugarrrrrrrrrrr in particularrrrrrrrrrrrr.*"

"Who doesn't," barked Beanie. "You aren't the only one!"

"*Ooooowwww,*" the darkness groaned. "*I thought I was the one annnnnnnnn only. I thought I was the only one who rrrrrrrreally really mattered.*"

"Well, you're not," shouted the pug.

"*I don't know how I came to beeeeeeeeee,*" it went on. "*I can't even seem to mooooooove. I'm stuck under here. And not one flower likes me. They all shudder and turrrrrrrrn away. How do you think that makes meeeeeeeeeee feel?*"

"Like you-know-what," barked Beanie. "Careful not to step in it!"

"Why don't you lighten up a bit?" Lee suggested. "Why don't you try to relax."

"*Eeeeeeeeeeeeeasy for youuuuuuu to say,*" groaned Spigot-Von-Glume. "*I do not like sssssssuggestionsssssssssssss.*"

It was as if this dark cloud had not been given the chance to speak for such a long time, it wanted to unload a terrible burden. "*I don't knooooooow why I'm like this. What have I everrrrrrrrrrr done?*"

"That might be just the problem," grumbled Garbonzo. "What have you ever done for anyone else?"

But the Glume didn't seem to understand this, and went on in its own dark vein. "*I don't fit in. I don't belonnnnnnng. I can't help but smotherrrrrrrrrrrr everything.*"

"Why do you smother?" the pug dog asked. "Are you a rug?"

They were all trying to understand what was wrong with this gloomy being. How could anything be so miserable?

"Have you ever tried to contribute?" Marvel asked.

"*What do I have to givvvvvvvvvve?*" responded the Gloom. "*All of the flowers were having sooooooooooooo much fun. I couldn't stand it, all that noise—dancing and singing all the time—It was like one big party and no one had even invited meeeeeeeeee. They never dooooooooo.*"

"Boo-hoo," the pug responded.

"Have you ever invited anyone anywhere?" Marvel asked.

"*They wouldn't come with meeeeeeee,*" responded Spigot-Von-Glume. "*They don't liiiiiiiiike me. I'm not niiiiiiiiiiiiice. I can't help it! I feeeeeeeeeeeel rotten... and I say bad things.*"

"So do I!" yelped Beanie, "and everybody likes me fine!"

But Bonzo gave him a push with his paw to keep him from interrupting. Let this dark Glume speak and get whatever it was off its chest.

"You must be ill," Marvel continued.

"*Verrrrrry, very ill. In morrrrrre ways than onnnnnnnnne.*"

The more Marvel discoursed with Spigot-Von-Glume, the more condensed its presence became, so that the dark fog didn't seem to take up so much room—it was flattening out, and becoming more of a sticky-looking liquid. They could almost see the golden Pink Cloud of Perfection twinkling high above them now, as if She were hovering over the entire garden.

"*What is yourrrrrrrrrrr name?*" the Glume inquired.

"Marvel the Marvelous," the purple pony replied with a cheerful nicker.

"*Ohhhhhhhhhhhhhhh, you must be quiiiiiiiite popular. You wouldn't like me at alllllllllllllll.*"

"Why wouldn't I? I like you fine."

"*I come out of that nasty faucet, and I stick to things. If you really wanted to help me out, you would turn that spigot OFF–turn me off foreverrrrrrrrrrrrrr. It would be such a relief, to everyone.*"

They could see the tar-like sap dripping from the garden faucet. "If we turn it off, would that be the end of you?" Marvel asked.

"*Oh, no no nooooooooo,*" it moaned. "*I connect to something else, much much bigger. Something AWFUL. Faucets connect through underground pipes. I have a source—I'm sure of it, and it's probably poisoning the entire world.*"

The more Spigot-Von-Glume spoke to them, the more concentrated it became, so that they could see a kind of form that was caught beneath its sheet of liquid tar. It seemed to be down on all fours, and it rocked from side to side, obviously hard for this sorrowful being to move beneath the presence of its sticky, dark covering.

"You look trapped," said Beanie, and with this the Glume gave a very deep sigh, and then a radical hiccup, which was the best it could do for a positive response. "*You've named it, little dog. Thank you for your sincere diagnosis. It makes me feel better somehow.*"

"You're welcome," barked Beanie, exceedingly proud for doing his part.

"I think Beanie is right," Lee added. "Spigot-Von-Glume is a kind of prisoner."

"*Yes,*" it answered, "*a poisoned prisoner. But what will prevent me from passing it on? Everything is suffering. Probably because of me.*"

"Probably not," said the mastiff. "You're not the source of all misery."

"*What issssssssss, then?*" Spigot wanted to know.

That they did not know.

Marvel was still thinking about the faucet and whether they should try to shut it off—would that be the same thing as killing this creature? That wouldn't be right. Or was that the only way to release it from this living torture?

"*I'm not sure if there can ever be an end to me,*" Spigot-Von-Glume confessed. "*I'm not sure there is an end, or a beginning forrrrr thaaaaat matterrrr. Just endlessssssss, drrrrrrreadful weariness. Everyone is just filling their days. Filling their daaaaaaysssss in infinite waaaaaysssss. It is such a wasssssste of time. But if you turn that spigot off, it might give me some relieeeeef. Maybe I could sleeeeeeeeeeeeeep, perchance to dream. I could use a break from all thisssss wearrrrry blearrrrrrry tirednessssss, trapped in the middle, you know...*"

"Better than being drugged," yapped the pug. "I just remembered. I had a dream. A terrible dream!"

"*Rrrrrreally?*" Spigot-Von-Glume seemed interested in someone else for the first time. "*What did you dream? I never dream! Please tell me your dream little dog.*"

"I dreamt we were being chased by an enormous house that wanted to catch us and squash us! I just remembered that now."

"*But you got away, didn't you?*" Spigot-Von-Glume asked with some hope in its voice.

"Apparently," answered the pug.

120

"*I nevvvvvvvvvvvvver get away*," it responded.

"Well, everything's not about YOU," barked the pug.

"Dreams aren't real," Lee explained.

"*If I had a dream, I would make it real. I would treasure it forever and ever. But since I can't sleep, I can not dream. Maybe if you were to turn off that faucet, I would be able to sleep and dream.*"

"Maybe you'd have a good dream, too," Marvel predicted.

"*Doubtful,*" said the Glume. "*But can you help me, please. Pretty please with sugar on it?*"

They all conferred and agreed that, Yes, they sincerely wanted to help.

Holding hands, they stood around the gloomy lump that continued to sway beneath its tar-like blanket, and as they united together, a soft pink rain began to fall from the soaring Pink Cloud above. The cloud swelled up, and as it sprinkled its pure, sweet rain light, it swept away the awful smell, and reduced the essence of the gloomy Glume to a flattened, sticky puddle. Its essence still bubbled beneath the surface, like a very-thin-someone in a kind of helmet, tossing and turning beneath the covers.

The entire group was immensely grateful for the mist of springtime air that the rain shower seemed to bring with it, refreshing the flowers a bit.

Spigot-Von-Glume continued dribbling its terrible, dark substance, and Marvel knew she had to do something soon to shut it off.

Lee tried to turn the handle with both hands, but it wouldn't budge.

"Kick it," cried the pug. "Give it a good *whack*!"

"With all your might," added Bonzo, flexing his muscles to show what he meant.

Marvel got into position with both rear feet poised.

They could see the golden Pink Cloud retreating—twinkling with little opalites, sprinkling them down from the heart of Her Being. They came sparkling and floating down all around them and made them feel cheerful again.

Marvel put her hind legs to the dripping spigot and gave it an awesome *bang*. It seemed to move a little.

"*Once more*," whimpered Spigot-Von-Glume.

Marvel kicked a second time, and the handle turned. She was getting a rather sticky rump, but the force of her hooves was their only hope. She kicked it again, a third time, with an especially powerful *whonk*, and the black substance stopped its dripping.

"WHEW," cried the pug, panting and snorting. "We can breathe again. At last!"

Honey-Bunnies Lead the Way

*T*hey looked around, and saw that they were at the heart of Castle City. The place looked abandoned, with the exception of one golden-brown bunny who hopped tentatively in their direction.

"And who are you?" Lee countered.

"And who are *you*?" it answered.

"Are you an echo?" Lee continued.

"Are *you* an echo?" it responded. "Why *do* you ask?"

"Why do *you* ask?"

"I asked you first!"

"I asked you second."

"*First is worst*," put in Beanie, for he hated to be excluded from any conversation, especially a nonsensical one.

"And who asked YOU?" the bunny thumped.

"No one asked me, I asked YOU," Beanie replied. "Why do you talk such nonsense?"

"Speak for *yourself*," the bunny said.

"I was speaking for myself. You weren't!"

"What kind of creature are you?" Marvel asked.

"I'm a honey-bunny," it responded.

"More like a dummy-bunny," said the pug.

It pretended that it had not heard this last comment and replied, "I was just getting warmed up for a bit of a thump. I haven't thumped or bumped in over a fortnight."

"I know what that is, a fortnight!" yapped Beanie.

"Well, it looks like you've saved the day," the honey-bunny addressed Marvel the Marvelous, finally making some sense. "We were all about to expire without the good Queen's cheer. We're used to supping on sweetness, you know, and there has been nothing but sour fumes for over..."

"A fortnight!" yelped Beanie.

"In any case, we seem to have lost all track of time in the midst of this very bad weather. Do you think you could water the flowers for us?" the bunny addressed Lee.

Lee wasn't sure where she could find water, but the honey-bunny had an answer to that. He pointed to the rusty old watering can, and led them over to the dried-up pool which was now a pitiful pit. Then the bunny began thumping its foot on the edge, in a kind of bunny-thumping way. The sound was rather contagious, and they all began to clap in rhythm together—*Clap-clap Clap CLAP, Clapclap Clap CLAP.*

Soon a few more honey-bunnies appeared and they all did a thumping, jumping kind of dance on the edge of this dried up pit. Everyone joined in the dance as best he could, the pug holding his sore little paw in the air, hanging onto the bone bag with his scrunched up jowls.

Finally, after a whole lot of thumping and bumping, a geyser of clean fresh water shot up, and all of the honey-bunnies cheered in unison. *"It's back. It's back from Hackensack!"*

The Heart of Joya had returned to life! Thank goodness for life giving water.

Before long the circular pool was filled to the brim. It was a beautiful turquoise-blue, and the sky had become a luscious lavender again. The birds all began singing and cooing and trilling, and everything seemed like it might remain pleasant and good forever and a day.

"I wonder if I could clean myself off," Marvel asked the honey-bunnies. "I seem to be rather sticky."

"Better get that off your bottom," one bunny thumped, "before everything gets stuck to it."

Flower petals and pebbles and big flat leaves and pokey twigs had already begun to cling to Marvel's rump, and it was beginning to agitate her. Marvel rubbed her bottom against a tree in a desperate effort to get the black tar off, but bits of bark clung to her rear, which made her feel like pawing.

"Please don't soak yourself in the Heart of Joya. That could pollute our whole system."

"Your girl child can carry water in the can," the original honey-bunny directed.

"Excuse me, but my name is Lee. Or you can call me Leezie."

"What kind of name is *that*?" asked the honey-bunny with a hoot.

"I don't know," she admitted. "It's just a nickname."

"Sickname is more like it!" The honey-bunny thumped the ground. "Leezie sounds like Sneezie."

"Or Wheezie—it's too breezy!" the bunnies laughed.

"Her knobby knees, do not please!" They began thumping and rhyming in a kind of hilarity that no one else found very funny. In fact, Lee was beginning to feel quite sensitive.

One thing all creatures seem to have in common, is that they don't like others making fun of their names. It was possible to do that with almost anyone. Her friends joined in to prove that point.

"I'm Marvel the rolling Marble, and I can warble."

"My name is Beanie, and I'm no Weenie!"

"You're a Dumb Bunny 'cause you think you're funny, when you're nose is runny," barked Bonzo.

The honey-bunnies seemed to quiet down after that.

"I do believe your watering can is rusty," Lee said to them in her most polite manner, so as not to agitate them any further. "I don't think it could possibly hold enough water."

"Doesn't hurt to try," said the leader of the honey-bunnies with a hoot.

"Trying is better than crying," they all laughed in unison.

"Better than dying by frying," another shrieked hysterically.

Lee wrinkled her brow in consternation. "It's not a matter of trying," she answered. "Can't you see that this leaky old thing can't possibly hold any water?" But just to satisfy everyone, she dipped the watering can into the bright blue pool that was at the Heart of Joya, and the rusty container became sparkling new!

"A Miracle!" the honey-bunnies cried in unison, as if they had known the outcome all along. They thought this troop of travelers was awfully ignorant of the laws of Joya where everything was healed by water.

"I still don't think you should make fun of names," Lee reprimanded. "It's not funny. It hurts."

"But making fun is our job! And too much laughing always hurts." They thumped and bumped and laughed some more, and gave Lee a tiny tickle, and a little lovey-dovey push, wee bunny like kisses with their wiry whiskers, until she gave in and smiled, and they all laughed together. That did feel rather good.

"Teasing can feel as good as *sneezing*," one honey-bunny replied. "*AH-Choooo! Choo-choo.*"

The honey-bunnies all got into a long line and began to do the bunny-hop, two hops forward and one hop back, popping around the garden.

"Did you tease old Spigot-Von-Glume?" Bonzo asked.

"Oh *nooooooo*," they responded together. "Glume is doomed!"

"You see! They didn't include poor Glume, and so it felt bad. You could have said—*Make room for Glume*, or—*Give him a balloon*," Lee added, as she carried the watering can over to

Marvel, and sprinkled the matted rump. This gave the purple pony much needed relief. While Bonzo scrubbed Marvel down, Lee rinsed and poured and rinsed again.

"Just look at yourself! You almost look as good as a shiny purple plum."

"With a brand new bum!" sang the honey-bunnies.

"Or a purple potato from Peru," barked the Pug, who seemed to have been infected by all the teasing and nonsense.

"You're the one who looks like a burnt potato," said Bonzo.

"I do NOT," retorted the pug with a *snort, snort-snort,* which the bunnies found hilarious.

They even imitated the sound, *Snort-Snort,* as if they were some kind of train, chugging along, pulling each other right out of the garden—out through the bunny-sized garden gate, shaking their cute little tails behind them.

The rest of the party was almost glad to see them go, for everyone had had enough of their hilarity. It was exhausting.

"Why don't you help me water the flowers," Lee asked the pug. "You could make yourself useful."

"But I'm not a useful breed. I'm just here for decoration." He then gave a couple of scolding barks, for he was the Queen's own darling dog. He belonged in her lap and nowhere else.

"Well, the Queen would be despondent if she saw what has happened to her beloved garden," Lee reminded him. "And the King would have a fit!"

"That's right," barked Bonzo. "We can't have that. We had better help bring everything back to life before the King returns.

He'll probably be coming along shortly." Bonzo knew that the King (crown or no crown) hated to miss out on anything.

So they all pitched in and helped revive the flower garden. Lee carried can after can of welcomed water to each of the flower beds, and sprinkled the thirsty, reviving flowers.

Soon they were surrounded by the prettiest garden you have ever seen. The flowers, refreshed, began to dance all around. The roses told the purple pony that she was almost like a flower too. "We think you are *very* beautiful."

"Are you a Gladiola?" one little Peony ball asked. "You look so happy!"

"Maybe we're cousins," a tall, elegant Delphinium spoke up. Though she was a pale blue, she had heard there were also purple-colored relatives in her flower family. She wouldn't have minded being related to Marvel.

"I want her in *my* bouquet," cried a tiny Viola.

"Marvel is not a flower," Beanie reminded them all. "Can't you see that she's a horse?"

"Marvel the Marvelous," Lee added.

Marvel did a deep equine bow before them all. "And this is my friend Lee Rumsey."

"*Best* friend," Lee corrected.

"Yes, *very* best friend," Marvel said.

But somehow Lee wondered if she was just one more friend out of all the others. It was as if her heart were slightly tainted by Spigot-Von-Glume. Some kind of strange, lingering sadness hung on inside of her. The good feelings she had for Marvel

were now mixed up with a bittersweet ache. Lee was confused. She didn't know where she wanted to be or what she wanted to do, but at that moment, she thought she heard her baby sister crying not too far away.

"We are trying to find the Treasure House," Marvel continued, "so that Lee can get home to her family."

This also made Lee feel strangely sad, for weren't Garbonzo and Beanie, Marvel and all the creatures of Joya part of her larger family too? Did she really want to leave this sunny, beautiful garden? Did she want to leave her best friend behind?

"Does the Treasure House even exist?" Beanie asked.

"Don't say that," the Delphinium scolded.

"Indeed, it's *very* real," the flowers trilled in unison. "We should know. We helped build it." But something was holding them back. They were not telling all.

"Is it somewhere around here?" Bonzo queried.

"Can you help *us* out for a change?" added Beanie.

Marvel whinnied. "We would be very much obliged."

"We can help you, certainly," said the Delphinium, "but I'm not sure we'd be doing you much of a favor. You might do better to just stay here with us. But if you want to know the truth..." the flower hesitated for a moment.

"We'll whisper it to you," added a tiny Viola.

Then all the flowers became silent and still. One little rosebud put a leaf to her mouth, and the Violets seemed to shrink back.

"What's wrong with you?" demanded the pug. "Speak up for heaven's sake!"

"Yes-yes," piped up a friendly Dahlia, turning to the tall Delphinium to let her finish.

"The Treasure House exists," she murmured, "but there is something terrible blocking the way. And none of us has been able to get around it, or under it, or even over it, not for a very long time."

"So you've been blocked?" Marvel assessed the situation.

"Yes," the Violets trilled.

"Blocked by the Darkling Orblock! It can suck your soul right up."

"It's very Big and it's *very* BAD and–"

"For heaven's sakes!" pronounced the pug. "It's always something, I tell you."

On the Right Path

On the other side of the garden gate, Lee and Marvel found a path that wound its way down the mountainside, down towards a grove of birch trees and a little jubilant creek.

Garbonzo and Beanie took two peeks at the descent, and decided that they would stay behind. They had both had enough ascending and descending for a while. "We'll wait until the King and Queen arrive. Then we'll bring them along," they promised.

"We'll come as fast as we're *able*," Beanie added, "considering some of us are badly wounded. But do take this," he offered his bone bag. "It might come in handy." The heavy bag was getting a bit bothersome, and clearly he was tired of dragging it around.

"Why thank you, Beanie," Lee took his little paw, and saw that it was all wrapped up by a pink gauzy bandage. The pug would be dancing in no time, she thought. Even that idea made her slightly morose, for she would miss him terribly. No matter how badly she felt, Beanie always made her laugh, the imp.

"Don't do anything I wouldn't do," Beanie twirled in place, stopping to make a little bow.

The mastiff turned toward Marvel and Lee. "I hope you find what you're looking for."

This comment made Lee a bit worried. Surely some part of Spigot-Von-Glume could be turned on and off inside a person. She felt she was carrying a bit of Glume along inside her. She couldn't shake it.

The sad part was that she no longer knew *what* she was looking for. Was she looking for happiness? Did she really want to go home? Did she want to sing and dance, like the flowers in the garden, or did she only want to wake up in her own warm bed with her soft, stuffed animals? Did Marvel love her as much as she loved her friend, or was this purple pony only taking her to the Treasure House to be rid of her? Marvel could head back north, where nobody ever cried (except perhaps the smallest flowers). If Marvel could leave the dogs behind, Marvel could ditch her too!

Lee realized this last thought was pretty unfair, but she had somehow begun to doubt her friend, and that felt terrible.

"I think I'll walk," Lee announced, getting out of the saddle, holding the reins rather carelessly behind her. She wouldn't even look at Marvel for fear of bursting into tears. Lee was sure now that Marvel only wanted to go home to find a proper partner. Maybe the Lippizans had a handsome, young brother, and they could all be a big happy family of four-footers.

Lee became very quiet, and Marvel gave her a nudge with her velvety nose, trying to jolly Lee out of this mood. Marvel's presence usually served to cheer Lee up, especially when she put a hand under the pony's golden mane, like that time, so long ago, when Marvel had helped to thaw her out.

"What's wrong? Do you need a little nibble from your purple plum?"

"I'm sorry," Lee apologized. "I was having bad thoughts."

"*Friends, friends, til the end*," Marvel sang to cheer her up.

"That's just it, THE END. I don't want to think about anything ending."

"Well, then don't," Marvel answered abruptly. "Think about new beginnings. Because every end has a brand new start. They link together, you see?"

No, Leezie didn't see. And Marvel couldn't explain it further.

For some reason the creatures of Joya never worried about seeing their friends again, about making new friends, or losing them. No creature cried when someone left (although Beanie was known to scold). Everything flowed in a natural stream of events, and good friends always came around, just like the two dogs had showed up in the middle of the garden, just as the King & Queen were bound to arrive any day now and there would be a joyful reunion, just as the Heart of Joya had come back to life from a dried up hole to a spring full of water. One simply had to trust in the cycle of things and not be too impatient. *Snort-snort.*

But Lee's black mood was oddly contagious, and soon Marvel began to feel awful. Marvel's heart was getting so heavy it was like a soggy old sponge that had taken in too much black water—her spirits were sopping wet. Marvel hung her head as she walked along and dragged her feet complaining, "I'm all worn out."

"Tiredness can make one grumpy," Lee admitted. That's what her mother always used to say, and perhaps her Mom was right. Lee was tired too and feeling nasty.

"At least we're not alone," Marvel added. "I don't mind being tired if you are too."

"Yes," Lee stopped to lean her head against her friend's golden mane. "I feel safe when I'm with you."

After that, they both felt a little bit better. Together, they followed the switchbacks down the mountainside, first this way, then back and around, until Leezie almost felt dizzy with the descent. She looked way out into the distance and saw what a beautiful place Joya was, with its Deep Dark Woods and rugged mountains, its lovely valleys and sparkling streams. It almost hurt Lee to look out over it all, knowing she would soon be back to normal, flat city streets and fenced-in yards.

She gazed down at the path and tried not to stumble. She felt as if she were getting careless. "I never thought that going down could be this difficult."

"It's certainly easier than climbing," Marvel added.

"Especially when you have to carry me."

It seemed she wanted to argue about everything. Lee couldn't quite explain it, but she almost wanted to fall down hard and bang her knee so that Marvel would have to make a fuss over her. Lee realized that she didn't want to go, but she felt like she had to now.

Marvel wondered if she was traveling with Sister-Von-Gloom, or if Lee had been infected by that sticky creature. Marvel remembered that talking was the only thing that had helped poor Spigot, so she tried to keep conversing.

"What would you like to do right now?" Marvel made small talk. "If you could do anything, anything at all, what would it be? Would you like to go back to that beautiful pool where we swam amongst the flowers and butterflies?"

"I'd like to take our time," Lee admitted. "I don't know why we're in such a rush. Are you just trying to get rid of me as soon as possible?"

Marvel neighed—"What a thing to say! I'm just trying to help you, silly."

"Well, maybe we could rest somewhere. I'd love to just lie down for a bit."

"I'm glad to hear that," Marvel responded, "because frankly, I think we need to rest up, so that we're in shape for whatever it is we're going to meet."

"Which is Very Big and *very* BAD," Lee repeated what they had been told. She wondered what a soul-sucking monster would look like. She wondered if they would be able to get past it, or would it simply inhale them, or squash them like bugs.

"This looks like just the place," Marvel announced as the path became level near the burbling brook.

Lee dismounted and undid the saddle, so that they could rest. The water was delicious and clear, and they both drank their fill until it revived them. It smelled like the forest, and river stones.

Peering down, Lee began to gather the prettiest stones until she had quite a collection. They were brilliant, almost dazzling under the water, but as soon as they began to dry, they became somewhat dull. She had to keep splashing them with more and more water. Lee imagined that her life would change in much the same way, from jewel-like stones to plain old rocks, but she didn't want to think about that now. She simply wanted to play.

She stacked the stones, one on top of another, until she had made a tower. Then she built another beside it, even taller. Marvel joined in, and pushed stones over toward Lee with her muzzle. One tower toppled over onto another and they both laughed, collapsing onto the grass. They rolled, side by side, scratching their backs, and then looked up at the sun that was filtering through the treetops.

It was a beautiful late afternoon, so balmy and warm, just the right temperature. The grass growing on the banks of the stream was delicious, and even a few ripe strawberries were hidden here and there. Lee picked a handful and fed them to Marvel, and then helped herself to some berries as well.

Marvel licked the red juice from Leezie's hands. "That tickles!" Lee laughed.

Finally, they both felt better.

As the moon began to rise, and the sunset gleamed across the sky with slashes of orange and pink and purple, Lee curled up with her arms around Marvel's neck, making a blanket of the golden mane. Pulling it over her shoulder, Lee felt happy and cozy. She didn't know why she had doubted her friend. Together they fell into a delicious slumber where their quiet breathing seemed to match each other's. Both of them had very sweet dreams.

Sound asleep, they didn't see the hover of *opalites* which had followed them out of the garden and down the path.

Marvel dreamt that she was swimming in that springtime pool, but then she rose from the water as if she could fly, and she flew over Northern Joya. Down below she could see her two pink sisters, who didn't look quite as beautiful or elegant now, with their herd of patch-work ponies climbing all over them, pulling on their manes. The big white Lippizans grazed together, apart from the sisters, who seemed to be doing most of the work. That didn't seem fair to Marvel, and she wondered if her sisters were truly happy. But then Marvel found herself running away on the green grassy fields, running as if she were flying through clouds. It felt good to be flying away.

Lee dreamt that she held her baby sister, and that Claire was no longer crying, but waving her little hands and cooing, making happy gurgling noises that sounded very much like the gurgling of the nearby brook. Lee kissed the soft damp skin of the baby's palms and the baby leaned forward to kiss her back. They played peek-a-boo and giggled. Lee was relieved that Claire was as healthy and happy as ever all wrapped up in the softest flannel that was the color of creamy milk.

142

When Lee awoke, she felt as radiant as all the flowers in the garden, after they had been revived. She wandered about collecting wild flowers, and then braided them into Marvel's mane.

"I wish I could put flowers in your hair," Marvel said, "but my hooves don't seem to work that way."

"I'll do it for you," Lee responded, tucking a daisy behind her ear. "How's that?"

"Fetching!"

They both laughed. Lee put her arms around Marvel's neck. "I'm sorry I was in such a bad mood. I'm better now. I had a good dream."

Marvel said that she had dreamed of running through clouds, free and wild without saddle or bridle.

"Would you rather run that way?" Lee asked. She didn't

want her heart to turn sour again, and she tried to understand the feeling of freedom, what fun it would be to leap and fly, effortless and easy. She would always picture Marvel like that—full of life, a regal purple with a flashing golden tail and mane.

Marvel assured her that she liked riding double best. "You're my partner, don't forget. You're just the perfect weight, not too much, and not too little. Plus, you actually help guide me with your legs."

With that reassurance, Lee remounted, for she would rather ride Marvel than walk. The purple pony nodded her head up and down as Lee settled herself into the saddle.

"Are you ready?" Marvel asked.

"Ready to ride," exclaimed Lee.

So off they went, and as they moved on down the trail, they came to a field of Sunflowers, with their big round heads turned towards them. "Fine Day," the flowers sang in unison.

"Indeed," Lee responded with fresh resolve. "A good day to travel. I'm going home." She felt that she was very close to finding her family now. She wanted to make sure that everyone was alright, then maybe she could return to Joya. Maybe she could live in both worlds. She didn't think that she would have to choose.

The Dreadful Darkling Orblock

*T*ogether they followed the meandering bends of the river. The water almost seemed to sing to them as it passed around boulder and fallen tree, spilling down little waterfalls, gurgling and lapping and whooshing along.

The melting of Northern Joya had filled the river to the brim. It was so full, it seemed to sing, and Lee found herself humming along. Lee felt somewhat mindless as they traveled along beside the river, but soon, around midday, the path departed, and led them in another direction, away from the singing stream.

It wasn't long before they saw the crumbling ruins of a very old wall that was in great disrepair. It had at one time been painted with gold leaf, but the old mud bricks were peeling now. The forest grew thick and thorny behind the barrier, making it impossible to pass.

"Do you hear that noise?" Lee queried. She thought she could hear the same sucking sound she'd heard inside the tunnel—it was like a deep rumbling thunder turned inside out, as if it wanted to suck them both right up, as if it were a Great Big Emptiness, wanting and needing everything in sight.

Yes, Marvel heard it too, and had to struggle against the strange, sucking wind—for it wasn't like fighting against a true wind that swept up against you. Pieces of paper and old leaves went flying past them. Marvel had to lean back, trying to keep from being pulled into it. It was difficult to stay in balance. Lee leaned back in the saddle as far as she could to help her mount remain steady, but Lee's golden locks were sucked forward, obscuring her sight just as Marvel's mane blew forward, too.

Dropping the bone bag, Lee dismounted in one swift movement. Marvel told her, "Stay to my side!"

The sky was turning the color of split pea soup, and Lee wondered what would happen if it started to rain—would they get covered in putrid slime?

As they came around a sharp bend in the trail, both of their breaths were sucked up together, for there on the path, blocking the gate was a terrible looking, swollen creature. It was a yellowish-green and had a plentitude of long flaccid arms that were like vacuum cleaner hoses or waving tentacles. The dreadful, awesome, Darkling Orblock was firmly wedged into the opening. Where there had once been a golden passage, there was now only this amorphous form with a knobby head, prickly spikes pointing up from its topknot like nasty thorns.

146

As soon as the creature saw Marvel and Lee, its tentacles started whipping the air, as if it meant to snatch them up, or perhaps it was expecting to suck up a substantial toll. Whatever this thing was, its big blubbery mouth opened and closed, as did its squinty little eyes, for it had not seen any passersby for quite some time.

"Stand back," Marvel warned. "I'll talk to it." They both noticed a black hose screwed tightly into the monster's side, and wondered if that connected to the underground pipes that led to the garden spigot? Maybe it even connected to the tunnel system. There was a similar smell of rotting garbage.

Marvel and Lee kept inching forward, battling the sucking wind as they crept closer.

"STOP RIGHT THERE," announced the Darkling Orblock. More leaves and old newspapers and scraps of food flew toward the sucking monster. "NO PASSAGE WITHOUT PAY," it belched. "I DOUBT YOU HAVE ANYTHING I WOULD WANT, SO NO ADMITTANCE GRANTED."

Marvel thought about this for a moment, and asked, "Would you like our good will and good wishes?"

"NOT."

"Would you like an abundance of gratitude sent from the mammals of Joya?

"NOT."

"Would you like to take a break from your tiresome post? You must get weary standing there blocking the passage all the time."

"No, nay, never," it answered, as if to put an end to this conversation once and for all.

"Quite a contrary creature," Marvel whispered. "It only speaks in negatives."

"What did you say? No whispering here or you'll get fined and thrown into jail."

"We're just on a journey through Joya," Lee said, lifting the bone bag, "and we do have something precious."

It was clear that the Orblock was very interested, but all it said was, "Humpf. I doubt it's anything I would want."

"How do you know unless you see for yourself?" Marvel countered.

"Well, let me take a look," the Orblock responded, for indeed, it was rather boring sitting at the same post day after day with very few paying customers.

Lee opened the bag to take a peek, and even she was dazzled. A blast of golden light hit her face like a thousand dandelions all glowing with sunshine and liquid butter.

"What's that you've got in there?" puffed the Orblock. It seemed to stop its sucking for a moment, and got even bigger and greener and meaner looking with a new threatening curiosity. It was as if some kind of deadly fluid was writhing inside its stomach. The Orblock began to wave and stretch out its long, ugly tentacles, which oozed big drops of tar.

The dark liquid tar made Lee think about that poor depressed captive, and she couldn't help asking, "Do you know Spigot-Von-Glume?"

149

"WHAT'S IT TO YOU!" the Orblock blasted, sucking them forward a couple of feet.

"Well, if you want to see what's in this bag, you will have to let Spigot go. Spigot-Von-Glume is our friend."

"*HA*," the Darkling Orblock roared, as if it had never heard of anything so ridiculous. "SPIGOT-VON-GLUME IS NOTHING TO ME. YOU CAN HAVE ALL OF THE GLOOM YOU WANT!"

With this, the monster yanked the hose from its side—and immediately the long black hose began whipping around in the air like a nasty snake, shooting out a steady stream of sticky tar. Marvel had to dance back to keep out of the way.

Lee wondered if the tar fed the Orblock somehow. Was it like an intravenous feeding tube? But just as she thought this, there was a small explosion that burst from the end of the writhing hose—a burst of feathers gathered themselves into a lit-

tle ashen-colored bird, which circled three times above their heads, and began to twitter—*Thank you, Thank you, Thank you very much*, before it soared away.

Leezie waved and blew it kisses, so happy that Spigot-Von-Glume was finally released, and had taken the shape of a little grey bird that now could soar and fly away.

But the rumble of the Darkling Orblock brought her back to her senses. "SHOW ME WHAT YOU HAVE IN THAT BAG OF YOURS, OR ELSE!" the Orblock demanded. It was getting anxious, worried that the gold might disappear, and it had a terrible hunger for gold.

Lee wasn't about to argue. She put her hand down into the bag, and held up a golden bone.

The monster's eyes seemed to whirl inside its sockets when it saw the golden bone. But then it spoke, with obvious insincerity—"PROBABLY NOT WORTH MUCH."

Marvel knew that the Orblock was only trying to fool them. Gold was exactly what it craved. It would do anything to possess it. So Marvel countered, "We believe it is worth its weight in gold."

"WELL, THROW SOME OVER," the Orblock instructed, waving its tentacles greedily, reaching and stretching out for it.

"We'll throw just one at a time," Lee shouted back, still trying to overcome the sucking wind. "Do you mind turning off your vacuum?"

"WHATEVER YOU SAY," the Orblock responded. It was clearly trying to cajole them until it could get its hands on every single golden bone in that bag. Then it would probably try to snatch them up as well, but they had to go through with their plan. Maybe the Orblock would consider the golden bones adequate pay and let them pass.

The first bone was obviously heavy enough. The tentacle that grabbed it dipped toward the ground as it wrapped itself around the treasure.

"ANOTHER," it demanded. It could not resist catching each glorious bone. "ONE MORE," it yelled, then, "AGAIN!"

One after another it caught the bones until all its tentacles were weighted down. With a huge groan it lifted them up, as if they were golden barbells.

The Orblock seemed almost satisfied. "IS THAT ALL?" it blubbered. "AREN'T THERE ANY MORE?"

Lee stuck her head down into the bag, and saw that there was one more golden object at the very bottom—but it was a golden apple. It looked good enough to eat. "We've got one more thing." Lee told the Orblock. "But you don't seem to have any more hands. This one is really special."

"WHAT IS IT?" the Orblock wanted to know. "I NEED ONE MORE THING TO LET YOU PASS."

Lee held it up—A Golden Delicious.

But Marvel whinnied, "You don't have any more hands."

"I'LL CATCH IT IN MY MOUTH!" The Darkling Orblock puffed itself up, so that it became even more rotund, stuck firmly in the opening. Lee wondered how they would ever get around it, or if it would remain true to its word.

Lee looked at Marvel who nickered softly, then leaning back, Lee tossed the apple as high as she could, and the Orblock opened its big, blubbery mouth to catch the golden orb—but instead of snatching the apple with lips or teeth, it swallowed the golden apple whole. The apple slid down the Orblock's throat and lodged firmly in its windpipe.

It could not swallow or even breathe. Its eyes began to spin and grind as if they were sharpening invisible knives. It could not suck up any more air, and began scrubbing its weighted tentacles about on the ground in furious desperation.

Frantic, unable to dislodge the apple, its bulging eyes seemed about to burst, but still the Orblock held onto its bones as if they were a matter of life or death, and it had chosen the later.

Lee's first impulse was to rush forward and try to help, but Marvel held her back. This might be their only chance to get past the greedy monster.

With supreme velocity, Marvel reared up and leapt directly at the swollen creature, but the Orblock saw the purple flash and shot out a tentacle, wrapping the purple pony up with its long, rubbery arm. It lashed the purple pony around and around, whipping Marvel back and forth in the air, as if it could snap her neck.

Lee was afraid that the Orblock might dash her friend against the ground, crushing Marvel's skull. She could see that Marvel was almost delirious from the whipping movement, but still the apple was stuck, lodged in the Orblock's throat. Soon it

would run out of oxygen. How long would the monster hold out? Could Marvel survive the whiplash?

Leezie didn't know what to do. She had to think fast—all she had was the empty bag. But then suddenly the little grey bird reappeared, and flew three times around her head—until Lee felt a golden spark right behind her eyes (*on the inside*)—Yes, she had an idea!

Turning her back on the monster, she grabbed up a couple of big grey stones and threw them into the bone bag. Then she turned and held the bag up high, waving the bag and yelling, "You didn't get everything, look! I'll give you ALL the rest. You can have everything! Just let Marvel go."

The Orblock paused for a second, glancing at the freshly weighted bag, and in that instant, Marvel wriggled free and danced away, out of the Orblock's reach.

Lee swirled the stone bag over her head and let the plain old rocks fall out.

This mockery enraged the Orblock. It was turning a muddy green now, and its eyes were whirling red, but still it hung onto its golden bones.

Regaining equilibrium, Marvel reared up, then leapt toward the Darkling Orblock, making a perfect arc. Marvel flew with supreme velocity, while the muddy monster wobbled about, running out of air.

If it had dropped the golden bones and pounded itself on the back, it could have dislodged the apple, but it wasn't about to give up its loot.

With a tremendous leap—hooves straight out, Marvel lanced the Orblock's belly. The golden apple shot out of its mouth, as the Orblock made a deafening explosion. A cloud of rancid fumes erupted and its rubbery skin blew apart into a million bits, settling on the ground like ashes. The stench of the thing almost blinded them.

Lee scooped up the golden apple and stuffed it in her pocket. Flying through the billowing clouds was the little bird, and now it too appeared golden. *"Thank you thank you thank you,"* it sang.

Magic words, Leezie thought.

Delicious Apples, Tasty Tears

A wind from Northern Joya came sweeping into the valley, and blew the ashes of the Orblock away. The abandoned golden bones were unharmed by the destruction, but before too long they were transformed into shining opalites, and they drifted up, high into the air, whooshing back to the golden Pink Cloud of Perfection that had undoubtedly sent them.

Lee dropped to her knees and breathed out an exhausted sigh of relief. The Darkling Orblock was truly gone. There was no more sucking sound. The air was perfectly still.

They had cleared the path, and now it was time to mount back up. Cautiously, they moved forward together. Marvel leapt over the rank, scorched pit where the Orblock had been wedged for so long. And then, in the distance, far on the other side of the gate, they saw the Treasure House gleaming.

As they trotted up to the door of the place, which was more

like a magnificent dollhouse, Lee thought, she was dazzled by
the jewel-like flowers that grew all around the door—they looked
like diamonds, rubies, and sapphires with translucent jade leaves
and crystal stems, sparkling and tinkling as they swayed before
her. She had never seen a garden made out of gemstones before,
and she wondered if she should pick one.

But as she bent, the golden apple fell from her pocket and

landed outside the Treasure House door. She decided it wasn't right to take one of the gem flowers. They were too beautiful right where they were, and then Marvel whinnied—"It's opening!" Lee knew that she had to go now. Without thinking, she dashed through the Treasure House door as Marvel whinnied after her.

Inside, she was struck by the power of light—it was like standing on the inside of a star. But as she adjusted, she could see a dazzling, radiant bird hovering near the ceiling. It looked like one of Joya's doves, but light poured off of it in all directions.

Just below the bird appeared something even more wonderful—her baby sister, Claire, cradled in a luminous sack filled with twinkling opalites. The dove continued to hover above her, but now streams of peach and rose-colored light poured down to fill the luminous sack as the baby gurgled and waved.

Claire looked perfectly happy, and Lee wondered if she could reach up and touch her, but when she stretched her arms up high, the luminous sac ascended, just out of reach.

Lee wondered why she had heard baby Claire crying throughout her journey, for now she looked perfectly content, just like the baby in her dream—gurgling and waving her hands—laughing the happiest river-like laugh.

Lee moved forward, transfixed by the sight of her baby sister, suspended so close, yet just out of reach. She stretched up her arms and jumped again, but the ball of light rose toward the ceiling—it nestled there for a moment, and then disappeared before Leezie's eyes.

"Oh my," Lee said. "*Oh my, OH MY.*" She looked around,

dazzled by the very white walls of a strange, antiseptic, hospital room. She was lying in a metal bed, reaching up for her father and mother. Her parents were both standing over her.

When they saw that their daughter was conscious, they burst into tears, and then laughter, and then started to weep all over again, as if they could not believe it. All their prayers had been answered. They hugged and kissed her, leaned back and looked, as if they could not get enough of her. Their daughter was alive.

Even Lee's brother rushed over from the window and gave her a great big hug. Then he handed her a present he'd been

guarding especially for her—a little stuffed animal that looked like a pug.

"I know him," Lee said to her brother. "His name is Beanie." But more importantly, she added, "I just saw Claire."

Her brother responded, "Claire died in the accident. It was so fast, she didn't feel anything."

"That's not true," Lee said.

Their mother began to weep again, and their father kept saying that it was all his fault.

"Claire isn't dead," Lee whispered. "I just saw her in the Treasure House. She's fine. She's happy, believe me!"

Her brother only said, "Weird."

They all knew that Claire had passed away at the moment of impact. Lee had been thrown from the car, bashing her head. They had been waiting for her to come out of a coma.

"I'm sorry I punched you," her brother apologized.

"That's ok," she answered, for she knew that she had been taunting him. It wasn't entirely his fault. She thought about those honey-bunnies and all their teasing.

Where were the creatures of Joya now?

It was too soon to tell them about Marvel and Bonzo and the deep dark tunnel with the terrible smell, and the ice fields and melting water, and how Marvel had changed from a pretty pink pony into something much more beautiful.

Her family couldn't quite believe that their baby Claire had been seen in some other world, but then as Lee turned her head, a sparkling opalite fell from her hair and clattered onto the floor. Her brother saw it, just for a second, before it turned into a plain old spoon. After that he almost believed her.

Lee had been so far away, no one knew what she had experienced, but they could almost imagine baby Claire drifting with the Pink Cloud of Perfection in a land that was *"on the inside."*

Back in Joya, Marvel stood at the threshold of the Treasure House and listened to the human sounds of laughter and crying on the other side of the door. Marvel knew it was not time to enter, but for the first time in her entire life she realized she had tears in her eyes—in fact, she could even taste them. All she could do now was to raise her head and trumpet a mournful whinny. She called over and over, as if to tell Lee that she felt so sad, torn in two. As she tasted her own salty tears, she wanted Lee to know it was happening. Marvel heard nothing in return.

Hanging her head, Marvel imagined that she would return to Northern Joya now, find her sisters, Luster and Brilliance. She would show them her beautiful purple coat, and they

would no doubt be astonished. Marvel was sure she'd find a bunch of little patchwork ponies, colts and fillies that would probably climb all over her and want to play silly games. They'd kick up their tiny hooves and squeal. But even these thoughts didn't pick up her spirits.

With her head down close to the path, she followed the scent of something sweet. There, by the Treasure House door, she saw the golden apple, which had turned itself into a piece

of real fruit. She picked up the golden delicious with her lips, and crunched it in half. It filled her mouth with an explosion of flavor—it tasted—it tasted like Love!

She turned back towards Castle City, and there were the King and Queen coming down the trail with Bonzo and Beanie following. Marvel nodded up and down in welcome, and they waved and cheered in return. A host of flowers led the way, and a long line of honey-bunnies streamed behind, hopping and laughing, falling over each other.

Marvel was glad to see them. They were her family. They were her friends. Then why was she crying? Why did she look back at the Treasure House door, and whinny to make your heart break?

Back on earth, Leezie asked her family to please be quiet. "Did you hear that whinnying sound?" Suddenly she was filled with terrible remorse. When she tried to get out of bed, she found she was attached to a bunch of tubes. "I need to go back to Joya, now!"

Just then her doctor walked into the room. He looked like a nice enough man, but he didn't understand her agitation.

"I have to go back right now!" she pleaded. "I didn't even say Thank You!"

"You don't have to thank me," he said very gently, speaking in a soft, low voice, taking her hand.

"That's not what I mean," she argued. "I have to get up." Couldn't they see that she was fine?

But the doctor disagreed. "You must rest now, my dear. You've had a severe head trauma. You're lucky to be alive."

She reached up and felt the bandage wrapped around her head. She knew it would do no good to struggle. She did have a terrible headache and she didn't know what to think now.

Her parents shook their heads, No, Leezie was not going anywhere. She had to rest and recover, right there in the hospital, and then there would be weeks of physical therapy. She was still delirious, they thought.

Helplessly, she whimpered, until tears welled up in her big blue eyes. If only she had known that Marvel was crying too, it would have made all the difference. Only in some other secret world did their tears commingle and remain as one. In the heavens above the world of Joya, a shower of rain-light fell. They would stay in each other's hearts forever, no matter wherever they were.

Marvel looked up and felt a piercing sadness, even as she nickered out to the blur of friends that were quickly descending the trail. She would have to tell them that Leezie was gone, and she was overcome, realizing for the first time what it was to be real in this truly marvelous world.

LAURA CHESTER has written many volumes of poetry, prose and non-fiction. Most recently, Willow Creek Press published *Hiding Glory*, the first in The Land of Joya Series, as well as two literary, photographic anthologies, *Heartbeat for Horses* and *Eros & Equus*, both with photographer Donna DeMari. Chester and DeMari also collaborated on the non-fiction book *Holy Personal*, as well as a book of prose-poems and photographs, *Sparks*. A few of Chester's other books include *Lupus Novice, The Story of the Lake*, and *Kingdom Come*. Her most recent book of short stories, *Rancho Weirdo*, includes the drawings of Haeri Yoo, Bootstrap Press, 2008. Chester lives in Patagonia, Arizona, as well as the Berkshires of Massachusetts with her husband, Mason Rose. www.laurachester.com

GARY A. LIPPINCOTT specializes in fantasy, historical, and children's book illustration. With a BFA from the Maryland Institute College of Art, he has been the recipient of numerous awards for his artwork at science-fiction and fantasy conventions. His paintings are now collected worldwide. A member of the Western Massachusetts Illustrators Guild, Gary has exhibited at a wide variety of galleries and museums. His masterful watercolors grace the covers of many books, including *A Tolkien Miscellany, Earthsea and the Other Wind*, by Ursula K. Le Guin, *Little Big, Jeremey Thatcher Dragon Catcher*, as well as *Hiding Glory*, first in The Land of Joya series. Currently he is collaborating with Jane Yollen on a picture book, *Off to the Fairies Ball*. He lives in Petersham, Massachusetts. www.garylippincott.com